DANIEL

 and

ESTHER

DANIEL
🌿and🌿
ESTHER

Patrick Raymond

Margaret K. McElderry Books
NEW YORK

First United States Edition 1990

Margaret K. McElderry Books
Macmillan Publishing Company
866 Third Avenue
New York, New York 10022

Copyright © 1989 by Patrick Raymond
First published in Great Britain in 1989 by Hutchinson Children's Books

Printed in the United States of America
Designed by Barbara A. Fitzsimmons
10 9 8 7 6 5 4 3 2 1

Library of Congress Cataloging-in-Publication Data

Raymond, Patrick.
Daniel and Esther / Patrick Raymond. — 1st U.S. ed.
p.   cm.
Summary: In 1936, while attending Dartington Hall, an English
progressive school, thirteen-year-old Daniel meets Esther, a
slightly younger classmate who, as the years go by, becomes the
focus of his life.
[1. Boarding schools—Fiction. 2. Schools—Fiction. 3. Love—
Fiction. 4. England—Fiction.] I. Title.
PZ7.R218Dan 1990   [Fic]—dc20   89-49588   CIP   AC
ISBN 0-689-50404-3

*For Christopher
who knew Dartington*

❧ Note ❧

Dartington was a real school. In the 1930s, when this story takes place, it was one of the first to believe in freedom for young people, which seemed revolutionary at the time.

It is perhaps worth pointing out that, generally, the founders and the members of the staff are real people who have been given their own names; the children, however, are fictitious, though inevitably they have some ghostly forebears. The story of Daniel and Esther is not entirely untrue.

P.R.

DANIEL
and
ESTHER

1

ESTHER HAS GONE, AND WHERE SHE IS AT THE moment I have no idea. Beside me there is just a hollow space, just air. I can't even look at myself in the mirror because then I can see that I'm alone. I can't write her a letter because I've nowhere to send it. All I can do is repeat her name, but now I've done it a hundred times it sounds silly, and even when I change it to *Esther I love you!* it's not much better. Of course, at Dartington they taught us to think rationally and not to have stupid dreams, and I'm sure they would tell me to face the fact that Esther is in Europe, I am in America, and the war has begun.

Three years ago, in 1936, the Dartington school summer camp was at Scabbacombe Cove, which is near Brixham in Devon. Our tents were some way up from the sea in a narrow valley with a stream running down one side. A group of younger children from school had their camp below ours and closer to the beach. We could hear their voices most of the time because usually they were screaming. Esther was there, but I didn't notice her at first.

I remember how we raised the big bell tent, which was to be the camp's community center on a level space by the stream. A woman called Miss Franklyn had joined us recently as an assistant housemother and she took charge of putting up the tent. She had close-cut hair, canvas shorts that stretched below her knees, and a whistle dangling on a cord. We didn't like Miss Franklyn. We said she had no place at a progressive school where we called the staff by their Christian names and there were no rules to speak of. She used the whistle frantically as the tent swayed up. Of course, we pulled too hard on our side and the tent lurched toward us, Miss Franklyn going up on the other side. She said, "Oh, dear, you must obey the whistle! Now then— *again!*" It took us an hour to raise the tent and by then it was nearly dusk and the last of the sunlight was going off the sea. We lit the campfire and sat around it in a circle.

"She must go," said Trudi, who was a Jewish refugee from somewhere in Germany. "In advanced education, for persons of this type there is no place."

"I'll cast a spell," said Martin. "She'll turn purple and then vanish."

Now we could hear the whistle down at the beach. Miss Franklyn was calling the younger children back to shallow waters.

"A spell of diabolical potency," said Martin, who always spoke like that.

Trudi looked away from Martin, disgusted. "Her place

2

would be at a conventional girls' school. There they do not mind about these whistles."

"She's coming up from the beach," I said. In the fading light I could see her stumpy figure climbing the hill. I heard her laughing. I believed she liked it at Dartington.

"Can you really do it, Martin?" asked Walter, the village boy who paid no tuition. "I mean, can you?"

"I shall need powerful agents."

"Something dead?"

"Not quite dead."

Bella fell back into the grass, sniggering. She was a large girl with a bust you could already see. "Miss Franklyn has been converted to modern education," she said knowingly.

"How do you mean?" asked Walter, but Bella didn't say.

When Miss Franklyn drew level with us, we just sat there in silence. Bella tried not to laugh and choked. I could hear voices down at the cove as the staff and children took their clothes off and ran into the water. The voices of the younger children were still farther off.

Miss Franklyn dived into her tent and I saw the canvas rocking as she moved around inside.

"Just you watch," said Bella, dying with laughter.

A minute later Miss Franklyn threw open the tent flaps with a swagger and stepped into the gray light. She was naked. She put her hand across her mouth, suddenly embarrassed, but then she jumped in the air and ran down the meadow toward the cove, weaving between the nettles. At a point where the shadows began, I saw—though the others didn't—how she leaped a clump of thistles. I saw her rising up. I saw her leveling off just where the highest thistle would brush against her bottom. Then, as the prickles touched her, I saw her surge *upward again*, without

3

putting a foot on the ground, and then disappear into the darkness where the valley opened on to the beach.

"The Dartington experiment appeals to Miss Franklyn," Bella said, and she rolled over and over in the grass.

"I'll cast a suitable spell," said Martin.

The staff were still on the beach and no one had told us to go to bed. I got up. I was sick of Martin and his spells.

"Where are you going?" asked Trudi, who could be bossy.

"Nowhere," I said.

I walked away from the others, thinking about Miss Franklyn. No one had told her we didn't blow whistles, take part in team games or use the cane. These things belonged in other schools, which we believed to be old-fashioned. This I knew better than the others because I'd been at such a school until they threw me out.

I went down the path Miss Franklyn had taken, coming at last to the beach. I could see the white bodies of the staff as they dipped in the water yards out. The younger children were silent now but just in sight. They were gathered round their housemother where the cove ended under the headland. I suppose Esther was there, but I hadn't seen her then.

Or had I? There was a child, a girl, standing a little way from the others where the sea was lapping the sand. She was kicking the water, sending up a little feather of spray. I liked the way she moved; she might have been dancing. I watched her for a long time as it grew even darker, with only the line of foam showing clearly. To this day I can't be sure it was Esther, but I think it must have been.

Bill Curry, the headmaster of Dartington, came to the camp next afternoon while we were shelling peas outside

4

the community tent. I saw him sitting on the hill above the camp, wearing a light blue suit and a sun hat. Below us, in a grassy hollow, the younger children were playing rounders. Miss Franklyn was there, blowing her whistle.

"Curry!" Martin called. "Come down here! I want to talk to you about Miss Franklyn."

(In fact, Martin had cast his spell the night before, using a broken comb, a ball of string, and a dead sea gull, but nothing had happened.)

The headmaster waved a small, fat hand and stayed where he was on the camp stool. Perhaps he wasn't bothered about Miss Franklyn. He was short and round, with a large head and small gray eyes. They said he was a mathematician who had become interested in "social harmony" or something like that. But he wasn't easy to know, and it may have been for this reason that we called him Curry and not Bill.

The basin was full of peas and I carried it to the stores tent and gave it to the housemother. From here I could see how the sun was shining in the bottom of the valley and making the sea bright in the cove. I went down the path, slowly. Where the children played, the grass was mixed with foxgloves and sorrel. Trees grew along the brook. I stopped in the shadow of the trees and watched the game. Once, the ball came in a long curve toward me and I caught it.

"Not out!" Miss Franklyn called. "Daniel isn't playing."

A dark girl, thin, quite small, had hit the ball. She put her tongue out in my direction to make it clear my catch wasn't allowed. Her black hair was shining and it moved all together, like a bell. Her legs were straight and brown. I watched her as she took another shot. When she swung the bat, her knees bent until her skirt touched the ground, but she gave the ball a tremendous whack all the same and it went winging out of bounds. I could see how determined her eyes were. She ran round the field so quickly she scored (but they'd lost the ball, actually) and there was some clapping.

"Well done, Esther!" Miss Franklyn said.

I don't know what came over me then; some sort of craziness, I suppose. At that time Esther was just one of the children whose shouts were filling the valley, and I don't think I was trying to impress her. I was more concerned about Miss Franklyn and her whistle.

I joined the game. I galloped onto the field, waving my arms up and down like wings. I ran round the bases, making great whooping noises and jumping in the air. Then I seized a blanket from the ground and ran after Miss Franklyn, holding it spread out behind her like a bath towel, and she ran away from me going "Oh—oh—*oh!*" I think the children were amused. Certainly Miss Franklyn looked funny as she bolted over the grass toward the stream. I made a lunge toward her, meaning to wrap her up in the blanket, but missed. She was going like smoke. I made another attempt to capture her—Daniel, the wild boy!— and this time I got the blanket over her head so that she went bounding away like a fat Arab.

I saw what was going to happen, even before it did. She came to the edge of the stream, took one step into nothing and came down with a great splash, the birds flying out of the trees above her.

There was a gasp, and then silence.

I tiptoed up to the bank and looked in. Miss Franklyn was wallowing about in the mud, crying. Then a lot of people came down from the camp, saying "How could he?" and "Poor Miss Franklyn!" Bella was there, giving me looks. They fished Miss Franklyn out of the stream and put towels around her. All I could do was stand there and watch, and wonder what I'd done.

I might have stood there forever but for Martin, who came down the path by the trees. He looked more pleased with himself than usual and I knew what he wanted.

He said, smirking, "Curry wants you, old pal. In the community tent."

I suppose I could have run away down the sands, but in fact I just nodded. Even at Dartington, when it came to it, we did what they told us. I walked slowly up to the camp. Curry was alone in the bell tent, sitting on a cushion, his knees drawn up and his little arms fastened round them. He wasn't in a temper or anything like that, but he kept his eyes away from me.

"You have been at Dartington—how long?" Curry asked.

"Only this term."

"And you are what age?"

"Thirteen."

"I understand that you started your education at a choir school, where you did quite well, but that you became unhappy when you went to another school."

If Curry wanted to do all the talking, that was all right by me.

"You didn't enjoy Haileybury, I believe."

"I was expelled."

"That needn't matter. To be expelled from a school is not necessarily disgraceful." Curry's voice was quiet and rather high-pitched. "Your parents thought you would do better in an atmosphere of tolerance and freedom."

I said nothing. My parents had separated a year ago and

now, as far as I knew, my father was in New York and my mother in France.

"They are, I believe, wealthy people."

"I suppose so."

Curry put his chin into his hands. "Why were you asked to leave Haileybury?"

"I punched a prefect. They said I was a problem child."

He nodded. "You may wish to know, Daniel, that in my belief there's no such thing as a problem child. Nor do I think that resistance to authority is necessarily a bad quality in a boy, particularly when, like yourself, he is not very tall. But that is a different thing from abusing the liberty you enjoy at Dartington."

He was getting at me for Miss Franklyn. "Yes," I said.

"We must think about your treatment of Miss Franklyn," Curry said.

"I didn't mean her to fall into the stream."

"But she *did*, Daniel. Your housefather tells me you have exceptional intelligence, even if you do no work. You could have foreseen the accident and the distress it would cause her."

I'd nothing to say, so I made a fizzing noise instead.

"There is much thoughtlessness in the world, much cruelty. Did you know that recently the Spanish army turned its weapons upon Spanish people? But no, you need not concern yourself with that. . . . Were you sorry when you saw what had happened to Miss Franklyn?"

"I was sorry when I saw her lying in the mud and rolling about. Before that, I thought she was just silly."

"What made you chase her across the field?"

"She was different. She wore a uniform and blew a whistle. Martin made a spell that was supposed to make her explode or something—"

8

"He did, did he?"

"—but I knew it wouldn't work. I thought it would be funny to wrap her up in a blanket. It was only when she started to cry that I realized it wasn't funny and just felt sick."

Curry was silent. Then he said, "I must tell you that Miss Franklyn was in any case leaving at the end of the term. Now she wishes to leave immediately."

I said, "Perhaps you'll ask her not to."

"Daniel, there is no reason why I should do your work for you. I have to confess that your behavior at Dartington, your wildness and your refusal to work, had led me to wonder if progressive education was suitable in your case. But you have shown me that you can be truthful and that you can recognize your own serious mistake. I will be satisfied if you will apologize to Miss Franklyn and ask her to stay until the end of the term."

"Is that all?"

"What more did you expect?"

"Some sort of punishment, I suppose."

"You must know, Daniel, that at Dartington we do not believe in punishment."

I went to the tent where Miss Franklyn lay flat on a camp bed. She looked like a burst balloon. She said nothing when I told her I was sorry, but I knew that she'd heard me; her hand lifted an inch in the air and waved about, which may have meant that she'd forgiven me.

"Please stay until the end of the term, Miss Franklyn," I said.

I went on to the hillside, feeling stupid. The afternoon sunlight was making gold flecks in the turf. The game had finished much earlier, though I could still see the footmarks in the grass, and the younger children were now somewhere else. I ran up to the top of the hill as fast as I could.

There I stopped. Below me, another valley opened out, where the grass was longer and wildflowers were growing here and there. The children were at the bottom of the valley, playing a silent game. One was hunting the others through the tall grass and shouting their names when he saw them. I sat on the hillside and watched.

I saw a shiny black head in the grass close by. Of course, it belonged to the girl I had watched playing ball. I tried to remember her name and got only as far as Estelle. (Estelle! *God!*) She was better at the game than the others. She kept still and very quiet, while the rest gave themselves away with idiotic dashes. Not English, I supposed, but that wasn't strange at Dartington.

I waved to her, but she took no notice. I shouted once and drummed my feet, and this time she looked up the hill, putting a finger to her lips.

"I can see you," I said.

She held her palm toward me and shook it from side to side, rubbing me out altogether. Her lips made huge, silent words, all of them angry.

A gull was rising over the headland. I dipped into the grass and crept along on my hands and knees. I couldn't see her now, only the yellow grass and the blue sky above, but when I listened I thought I could hear her. A rustle; nothing else. I turned in that direction and crawled forward, parting the grass with my head, feeling the sun's warmth and listening to the voices farther off.

We came face to face in a small hollow in the grass, where flowers were growing between the stems. She wasn't pleased, to say the least, but she made no effort to get away. I held her wrist with one hand.

"It's you again," she said. Her voice was low, with an accent I didn't recognize.

"Yes, me."

She was small. She was no more than a lot of black hair and chicken bones. When she turned her eyes toward me, I was surprised to find them cool and steady.

"You must let me go."

She spoke each word separately, as if they didn't come easily, which made her sound very serious.

"I won't. Ever," I said.

"You keep joining in games when you have not been invited. You spoiled our game."

"Who are you?"

She was damned if she was going to tell me.

"Actually, I know your name."

"Then why do you ask?"

"It's Estelle, isn't it?"

She said, "Esther." Then, much louder, *"Esther."*

A housemother was calling to us from somewhere nearby.

"Curry is most upset with you," Esther said. "You chased Miss Franklyn into the water. Why are you so awful?"

"I'm a problem child."

"That's a silly thing to be," she told me.

I hadn't let her go. I wanted to keep her here—here in the hollow of the grass where it was warm and no one else was in sight. Around us were the small noises of the undergrowth and further away the voice of the housemother, telling me to let Esther alone. A gull flew softly overhead.

11

My ears sang a little and I seemed to be dreaming. I remember that, of a sudden, Esther drew her fingers across my cheek, quite gently, her eyes very large and close, and that for a second or two she didn't speak.

Then, so quickly I couldn't stop her, she broke my hold and ran away, pausing once to look over her shoulder and put her tongue out, before disappearing somewhere down the hill.

❧ 2 ❧

THE SENIOR SCHOOL AT DARTINGTON, WHICH we called Foxhole, was built on the side of a hill which ran down a long way to the Bidwell Brook. There were woods on the lower slopes and a lane that dropped to the cider press at Shinners Bridge. After that, the hills of south Devon went rolling away toward Plymouth.

In 1936, the first summer of the Spanish War, the building at Foxhole was only about five years old. The houses where we lived were on either side of a large courtyard. Inside, the corridors smelled of polish and the sunlight seemed to come in at every window. We had separate rooms furnished in plain wood: a cupboard with a washbasin inside, and a low bed with a fitted cover. Everyone told us how privileged we were.

Above Foxhole, at the top of the hill, you could pass

through a gate into the gardens of Dartington Hall. There through the trees, very soon, you could see the gray stone of the Hall itself. It was as old as the school was new and was said to have belonged to a brother of Richard II. Mrs. Dorothy Elmhirst, an American, lived here. We met her sometimes in the garden, and then she would smile vaguely, put her head on one side and wander away. She owned the school and everything else, and we told each other she was the richest woman in the world.

There was a lot more on the Dartington estate, which a long bend of the river Dart surrounded on three sides. Beyond the Hall were the buildings of the arts, theater and music schools. At other places, you came upon studios and workshops and God knows what else besides. "Only provide the means of expression," the founders had written, "only give wings to the imagination, and social harmony will prevail." It was pretty crazy, I suppose.

We were not made to work, and I didn't, no matter that Curry told me I was wasting time and opportunity. In fact, I went on wasting time through the autumn. I spent hours in the woods, which always smelled of wild garlic. When the spring came, I did some work, but not very much. I went occasionally into the "creative workshop," which was a studio for those children who hadn't decided what they wanted to do. Here you could weave, model, or work in metal or wood. It was a bit of a mess, but I enjoyed it there. The studio was run by a Russian refugee called Oscar Ninsky, whom we nicknamed Ossi Nin.

Ossi's face was usually sad, but sometimes he would shout at the ceiling for no reason I could think of. "You, boy! You, Daniel! You do nothing with your time. You must *engage* yourself."

14

Once I took a lump of clay and worked at it with my fingers.

"That is something. That is good. Maybe you do not perish from ignorance after all. Now, an elongation of the neck. . . ."

But that spring I really believed that nothing was worth doing and instead I gave the figure ears like a rabbit.

"I cannot say what is this rabbit. You make fun of me, yes? You are a naughty boy puffed up with the winds of ignorance."

I remember how Ossi stood at my elbow, bearded, very sad, lifting his head for a final go at the ceiling.

"And one day you go *popf!*"

Esther lived in the junior house and I didn't see her much. In fact, I had almost forgotten her. I had even (can you believe it?) taken a fancy to another girl—or thought that I had—whom I saw one afternoon when I was looking from the window of the creative workshop, *only this girl turned out to be Esther as well!*

Beyond the window, a flight of steps led down to a sports field. The sunlight was playing on the grass. Children, strange children, came into the frame of the window and started down the steps. They were younger than I was. Among them was a girl in a blue coat whose face was turned away from me. Her coat was short and I could see the little dark hollows behind her knees. She was neat, awfully neat, and I wanted to go outside, run down the steps and look at her from the front. Then I realized it was Esther.

I left the workshop and went into the wood beside the sports field. I hid in the trees. The children were below me

15

on the grass, making long shadows, talking all the time. I kept them in sight as they passed into the wood and went down the steep hill toward the Bidwell Brook, which I could soon see shining ahead of them. Once Esther turned, as if she'd heard a sound up the hill, and I slipped behind a tree.

When I looked out again, she was a long way down the hill and paying no attention. She was shouting at the others and she sounded rather bossy. I went down behind her, from tree to tree, coming at last to the brook below the water mill. She wasn't there, though I could hear children's voices nearby. I sat on the grass beside the brook, alone. I could see the stream winding away between the trees, but nothing else.

For a long time there was nothing but the sunlight and the splashing of the stream.

Then, some way off, I saw Esther. She came out of the trees and went to the edge of the stream. She couldn't have seen me because a tree was in the way and I had to bend my neck to bring her into view. I think I was frightened of her. Me, frightened of Esther! I crawled forward and reached a spot where, lying flat, I could see her between the leaves.

She knelt down and looked into the stream. The water was almost still and her reflection was sharp. She looked just as good in the water as she did out of it. She leaned further out, where she must have been able to see her own face; perhaps she wanted to know how beautiful she was! I watched how her black hair fell forward on either side of her face, and how the sunlight, ruffled by the water, lit up her cheeks and sparked in her eyes.

I don't know how long I lay there, watching her. Once she looked into the trees beside the stream, and I knew that some of her friends were standing there. I heard Esther's voice across the water, clear as a bell, but the other voices were blurred.

"I'm going to Buckham's Barn," she said.

Whisper. . . .

"It's locked, of course. They won't give me the key."

Whisper, whisper. . . .

"I've got something there. Something valuable. I'll look in from the window."

Whisper, buzz, splutter, whisper. . . .

"I won't tell you what it is!"

Then Esther went away, walking slowly. She didn't want to join the others very much. She was too proud, too *refined.* She went into the wood and I kept looking at the place where she had disappeared, while the Bidwell went on running. I wondered what Esther had at Buckham's Barn.

After a time I got up and walked to the place where she'd looked into the water, and there I gazed at the shiny surface. I'd gone mad, I think. I was hoping her reflection would still be showing and I was disappointed when it wasn't. I stood on the bank for ages, watching the moving water, getting angry with Esther for being so neat.

Then, without thinking about it much, I took some stones from the bank and hurled them at the glassy surface, breaking it up, making flashes of light. I went on doing that for a minute or two. I smashed the surface so completely it reflected nothing but jagged pieces of the sun and sky, and then I ran away before it grew still again, going up the hill toward Foxhole.

The next day I went walking in the wood with Walter, the village boy, whose father was a gardener at the Hall. The warm days were just beginning, and under the trees I could see the first shoots of the bluebells and dog mercury. I led him to Buckham's Barn, which the school used as a storeroom. It was so old the wooden walls had turned silver.

Somewhere inside was Esther's secret possession, but I said nothing to Walter about that. We went in by a broken door and smelled the damp and the dust. At the back of the cow stall was another door, fastened by a padlock.

They won't give me the key, Esther had said.

"Jewels," said Walter, whispering.

"I don't think so."

We went outside, to a small dusty window through which we couldn't see much, just a hay-covered floor, some boxes and junk. The glass was cracked and it was an easy matter to push it through, but it made more of a crash than I'd expected and I jumped back. I found the inner catch and opened the window. The light was better now, but wasn't enough to fill the inside, where, a long way from the window, something large and black was standing.

"Help me in," I said. "I want to see what that is."

Walter doubled up under the window. I stood on his back, took the window frame in my hands and climbed in. Then, with my help, Walter got in as well, bringing down a cloud of dust. He was much too dense to be any good. We stood by the window and looked into the blackness.

Something valuable, she had said.

"Go on," said Walter, who was frightened.

I crept forward, seeing just the tiny threads of light that came down from the ceiling. My outstretched hands collided with cold metal and I pulled them back, catching my breath.

"We'd better go," said Walter.

18

I felt the object again, trying to decide what it was. "Guess what?"

But Walter wasn't thinking at all.

"An old car with a hood."

On the other side of the shed, high up, a curtain of sacking was covering a second window. When I pulled it down, the light showed us an open touring car with a ragged top.

So Esther had a car, probably left at Dartington by her parents. No wonder she couldn't take it outside.

I got in and turned the steering wheel left and right, making revving noises. After a while Walter joined me in the passenger seat.

I said, "We're off!"

"Burr-um!" said Walter faintly.

At that moment we heard a voice in the trees outside. No words, just a voice. Walter looked at me.

"The police," he said.

"How can it be?"

"I bet you."

We listened, our nerves jumping, as a footstep approached.

"A homicidal maniac," I said.

"No," said Walter, but he drew his head below the level of the door, all the same.

A shadow fell over the window and became still. Then slowly it crept forward. I pointed two fingers at the square of light. "I shall shoot," I said.

A face appeared in the window. A face screwed up, straining to see into the dark. Bloody Martin.

"Bang!" I said.

"What is it?" Martin asked. "Why all the noise?"

"Special racing car. We have plans for it."

Walter was bothered by that. "What plans?" he asked.

I couldn't tell him yet, because I wasn't sure. But I knew I could do something amazing with Esther's car, which she wasn't allowed to take outside.

"Tell me," said Walter.

No, not yet. First I had to get Martin through the window, where he got stuck, of course, and made a fuss; then I had to wait while Martin did the racing-driver bit at the steering wheel. But in those minutes, like a breaking-out of sunlight, I saw what I had to do.

"We're going to take it outside."

"But the door's locked," Walter said.

"That's just it. We're going to take it through the window."

"It won't go. Not nearly."

"It will, if we take it to pieces." If I had any doubts, they were lost in my excitement.

"That's silly," said Martin. "It would be easier to ask for the key and take it through the door."

"They won't give us the key. They're keeping it hidden. When we get the pieces outside we'll put them together again. It'll seem like magic."

Martin was sulky. Magic was *his* business.

"Curry won't be pleased," said Walter.

"He won't know until it's up again. Then he won't mind too much."

"All right," said Martin dully.

With my mind's eye, I saw the greased components sliding together on the grass outside. I saw the car complete, polished and shining in the sun. I saw Esther, her eyes lighted in amazement.

"Tonight," I said. "We'll borrow tools from the creative workshop and do the job by lamplight."

At that moment, I believed it possible.

"All right," they said.

When it came, the night was darker than I'd expected. The moon was covered and the wind was shaking the trees. We went down silently to the workshop. Tools: we'd need a lot of tools. We took one of everything and went out through a lower door. The wind cut my cheeks and found ways into my clothing. We took the lane to Buckham's Barn, where the trees stood close to the track, the branches waving, and it was even darker than before.

I switched on a flashlight and the beam showed me the front of the barn. The little window, lost in the gloom, was not so important now, and I had to remind myself why we'd come. I helped Martin and Walter to climb in, then I climbed in myself.

"Remember," I told them, "it's got to be a perfect job."

Martin had brought candles, which he placed at various points in the old wagon shed, but they didn't do much to lift the darkness.

"I'm starting at the back," I said.

I took a wrench to the spare wheel, and the retaining nut gave way, which encouraged me. (Daniel, the great engineer!) Then I carried the wheel to the window and pushed it out into the night beyond. Martin followed with the seat cushions. The only other parts to come away easily were the filler cap and the crank, and these we passed through the window.

"There's a lot of it left," Walter said.

I didn't want to think about that.

21

"S'pose it doesn't come to pieces. S'pose it's all stuck together."

"It *can't* be," I said. "They put it together, you see."

"Give me the wrench," said Martin.

He attacked the front of the car where the headlights were fixed to a tubular frame. He made a great deal of noise and only the glass gave way.

"Stop it! You're spoiling everything." I was desperate now.

"Nothing else to do, old sport."

"It *must* come apart."

"Only if you hit it in the right place."

Crash!

In an hour, working like mad, we had taken off the luggage rack, the cylinder head and various pieces of cable. One door fell off by itself. Walter then removed a handful of bolts from different places, after which we shook the body in the hope, I think, that it would fall into separate parts, each small enough to go through the window, but this didn't happen.

Martin was the first to give up. He lay on the floor, breathing heavily. "Not possible, old buddy. I never thought it was."

"You haven't tried yet."

"It wasn't *meant*, you see." It was like Martin to find a magic reason for doing nothing. "*They* don't want the car outside. And now they've started a storm *as well.*"

The wind had grown into a gale, it was true, and the trees were bending outside. There was a dreadful moaning in the rafters.

Martin held his hands to his neck and, using his feet, turned a full circle on the floor. "They've got me! They've got me!" he said.

A flash of lightning showed in the window. Thunder rolled round the edge of the wood. Walter came toward me, moving sideways.

"You said we'd have it done by now."

"Then get on with it," I said.

"The dreaded death rattle," said Martin. "Grrrr-aaa-hh!"

Walter said, "I'm tired. This isn't what I thought."

"Dead," said Martin. "Utterly dead."

We carried Martin, still dead, to the window and pushed him into the raging wind. He ran off at once, the shadows closing behind him.

I went back to the open hood. "Now we'll get it done," I said.

Then, the rain. It drummed on the old slates and came slanting through the window. Walter started again at the back of the car, but he was only banging the frame with a hammer.

After a while, he said, "The piece around the rear seat's all one. Even if we get it off it won't go through the window. I noticed that at the beginning."

"It will! It will! *It will!*"

He was silent for a long time. "No it won't."

He laid the hammer in the dust. He was pretty dense and in class he had difficulty in reading.

I said, "I thought you were a friend."

"We can't do it, Danny. I never thought we could."

(I didn't think we could, either, but I wasn't going to say so to Walter.)

I turned back to the engine. "Go, if you want to. I'll do it on my own."

Walter sniffed slightly and went to the window. He looked at me once, sadly, saying nothing. Then he climbed through and walked away without looking back.

Now the wind strengthened until it howled around the old barn. Every few minutes the window showed brightly as the lightning streaked across the sky. I worked under the hood, trying to remove the radiator. I know that I cried, and hurt my hands, but I went on pulling at the radiator while the storm raged outside.

"I'll do it, no matter what!"

One candle went out, then another. I was working in the dark with just the lightning to guide me. I wasn't thinking about Esther; now it was just a battle between me and the car, and I wasn't going to be beaten.

Then headlights blazed in the window. My name was called but I didn't answer. (Martin, of course, would have told them where I was.) I just leaned against the car, my hands on the radiator, and waited for them to open the barn and take me away. I hadn't given in. I'd just run out of strength. I heard the padlock being opened. Then a blanket was put around my shoulders and I was guided away.

Some words, I think. "You, boy! You, Daniel! It is foolish to work in the darkness when only the bats can see you."

I walked to the door, which now hung open. The storm was blowing itself out and the dark was broken by the first patches of light.

The voice again. "What a boy it is! What a brave and foolish boy! Now you come home with Ossi Nin."

❧ 3 ❧

THEY WOULD THROW ME OUT, I SUPPOSED, AND I wouldn't blame them. It had happened before. I remembered the stern white faces at Haileybury when they told me I was impossible. Once again the staff would get tired of making excuses for me and throw up their hands in horror.

The next day was Sunday, and as I couldn't believe they would expel me on a Sunday I left Foxhole and walked toward the river. I passed the Hall and the Chekov School, then I went down a lane that ended at a gate opening into fields. I stood looking over the gate. Beyond me, a track led downhill between trees. I couldn't have told you what I was doing there. I wondered if I could just vanish, leaving the earth in a beam of light, surprising them at Foxhole. I saw them standing under the clock tower, looking upward. *Just*

25

fancy, they were saying, *whatever happened to Daniel?*

A party of children was coming up the path from North Wood, making a lot of noise. They were led by one of the junior housemothers at Foxhole. A nature walk, probably returning from the Dart, where they would have looked for the Gadwell duck (or something) and not found it. I hid behind a tree while they passed.

A girl trailed behind the party. She was too superior to join them. I knew it was Esther even before I could see her properly. She saw me when she came to the gate, and she stood looking at me, frowning. I couldn't tell if she knew about the car or not.

"I'm Daniel," I said, expecting her to jump six feet in the air.

"My tooth hurts."

She put most of her hand into her mouth and worked it around a bit. Perhaps she didn't mind about the car. The other children were halfway down the lane, passing from one tree shadow to another.

"You've got a funny voice," I said.

She didn't reply, just hauled at her teeth with her thumb to make certain they weren't coming out.

"Where do you come from? It's not England, is it?"

"That is nothing to do with you."

Actually, I liked her voice, which was thick and low pitched, and I wanted her to say something else. Her English was much better now, though she still spoke each word as if she had to pay for it.

"You're a foreigner," I said. At that time I didn't mind if Esther liked me or not.

She darted forward and caught me a sharp blow on the ankle with the toe of her shoe. She owed me that for the

26

car. I took a pace toward her, but she backed away, once, twice, still facing me. Meanwhile, the others had reached the corner of the lane, where their voices faded out.

"You are just no good," Esther said, without much interest. "You are a problem child."

"I'm sorry about the car," I told her then.

"What car?"

"Your car."

"I haven't got a car," she said.

In the trees above us a thrush was singing. I tried to see him, but he was behind the leaves.

"I thought you had a car at Buckham's Barn," I said.

She looked at me sharply, drilling a hole through my head. "I have a bicycle at Buckham's Barn." Then she made the word ten times bigger. "A BICYCLE. But it's too big for me at present."

"Oh," I said. "I tried to take a car through a window. I thought it was yours and that you'd be pleased to have it outside."

Put like that, it sounded pretty loopy.

Esther snorted. She knew all about the two-seater in the barn, apparently. "The car you took to pieces belonged to Madame Oblomov at the Chekov School. I saw her going along with her hands in the air. Old Tatiana," she added.

"Oh."

She giggled. She was pleased to have cars torn apart in her honor, and she wasn't bothered about Old Tatiana. "How much of the car did you get through the window?"

"Not very much."

Then she was annoyed with herself because she'd giggled without meaning to. "What a stupid thing to do!" she said.

She ran down the lane without looking back. I followed

behind, but I was not as fast as she was, and a gap opened between us. She stopped in the shadow of a tree, turned toward me and glared. I stopped as well.

"Don't you touch me."

"I wasn't going to," I said.

I couldn't have touched her, anyway. She was different from me, someone who attended class, whose hair was brushed, whose clothes didn't come apart in the middle. She was ready to dash away faster than I could run. We looked at each other, panting.

"Why are you so silly?" Esther asked. "They don't have such people where I come from."

"What do they have, then?"

"Just children in class, wearing uniform. Rows and rows and rows."

I could see them all, dressed in gray, sitting there.

"Why don't you work?" she asked.

"Doesn't seem worth it."

"You must be very dull. A moron at least."

I knew I wasn't a moron, which was a favorite word at Dartington just then, like "endowment" and "complex." One day I would do something really brilliant, but I wasn't sure what it was.

"A low-grade moron with weak eyes. You will get expelled. Even Dartington does that. At night," she explained.

"I expect I will."

"They are never seen again, ever."

Actually, neither of us believed that.

Esther said, "It's disgraceful to be expelled. Where I come from . . ."

(That place again!)

"Yes?"

"Oh, they wouldn't put up with it. You would be taken away and . . . and reformed."

"How'd they do that?"

"By beating the soles of your feet with rubber mallets."

I wandered away from her, refusing to think about the mallets. I knew she was still behind me, leering at my back, but I went on for ten yards before I turned. She had stayed in the shadow of the tree.

"Go away," she said, but she didn't expect me to go.

She was passing her weight from one foot to the other, her little skirt rocking like a bell. She was in the mottled light under the leaves and she looked very pretty. She'd forgotten about the toothache. I took a zigzag path toward her, my head down, my hands in my pockets.

"You must be able to do *something*," Esther said.

"Oh, I can."

"What, exactly?"

I said suddenly, "I can sing, as it happens. I went to a choir school and I can read music." It sounded rather silly, so I added, "Not that I want to, of course."

She was revolving her toe in the dust, vaguely.

"They said I had a natural ear," I told her.

"You've got funny ears, actually. They curl over at the top. At home, there was a lot of music. When things got bad, I expected it to stop, but it went on."

I was annoyed with her for being mysterious, and I walked once around the tree where she was standing. When I came back to her, she was looking toward the dark mass of North Wood, and she didn't seem to mind if I reappeared or not.

"Can you bend over backward until you touch the ground behind you?" she asked.

"I don't think so."

29

"I will show you, then."

I wanted the trick to go wrong, which would make her less mysterious. It's difficult to be mysterious if you're a heap on the ground. But in fact she bent her body backward in one long movement and touched the ground with the palms of her hands, her hair falling. I could see the ends of her bloomers, which were the same reddish color as her skirt, and how the elastic had slipped up to show me where it had left a mark. She was thin, with bony hips and a flat stomach, but her legs were brown and smooth and in the sunlight they had a halo of fair hair. "You see?" she said, still doing it.

I pushed her stomach and she collapsed in a heap. She was very angry. I ran away down the lane while she called after me.

"You are awful—absolutely awful!" There was a lot more like that. Then she said, "They're going to deal with you. They've got a plan. You're going to be *reformed.*"

I ran straight into Esther's housemother, who'd come back to look for her, and she nearly went over backward.

"Oh, Daniel, Daniel," she said, gasping. "Why is it always you?"

When it came to it, Curry wasn't angry. He pushed the stem of his pipe into the hollow of his cheek, nodding his head silently. He was giving answers to questions he hadn't asked. We sat together in his study at Foxhole, which was a large, light room with windows opening onto the courtyard. Bridget Edwards, who was my group teacher, sat beside me on the sofa. Ossi Nin stood by the window, looking out.

Curry said, "Daniel, I have to admit to some indecision,

because in your case the fault may lie as much with the school as it does with you. You have done little work since you came here, and now you have damaged property not your own. As you know, we do not believe in compulsion, or in punishment, and try to achieve our ends by persuasion. But I am drawn to the conclusion that with you we have failed. Yet . . ."

Bridget, who was the only member of the staff to look like a teacher, touched my hand. I think she was on my side. She was a tall maiden lady with hair combed into a bun. "Daniel has intelligence," she said, "but so far we have not engaged his interest."

I sat with my eyes on the courtyard, listening to their voices. "You might as well chuck me out," I said.

Curry turned to me. I could not have said that he was smiling. His face was puzzled, his forehead lined, his eyes rather sad. "I could do that, Daniel, but nobody cares to admit a failure. You will not deny that you damaged Madame Oblomov's car."

"No," I said. But I added, "It wasn't much of a car."

"And now it is not even that," said Ossi. "I think he is made better by a heavy stick on the bottom."

Ossi had been through the Russian Revolution and he said things other people would not have dared to say at Dartington. Curry just smiled.

"You're not helping me, Daniel," Curry said.

"What help do you want?"

"Tell me about the car."

"It was just standing there. I meant to take it through the window and put it up again."

"You must have known that was impossible."

"I did, I think, but I liked the idea, anyway."

31

"Why?"

I said nothing; they could chuck me out before I mentioned Esther.

"Was there someone you were trying to impress?"

I moved my feet around, tying them in a knot.

"Am I right in thinking that Martin and Walter did only what you told them?" Curry went on.

"I suppose so. They weren't any good, as it happens."

"How did you see it ending?"

I wondered. "I saw the car outside, better than it was before. It would've been marvelous."

(I have to tell you, if I'm honest, that at one moment I'd seen myself driving off in the car with Esther beside me. I must have been crazy.)

Curry thought it over, rocking his head. He said, "I will accept, Daniel, that you had a purpose other than a destructive one. You may have been moved by creative exuberance."

All of a sudden, things were a little better. Somewhere the sun was coming out. Curry had satisfied himself that I wasn't a monster, but *creative*, and it was only Ossi who tossed his head.

"Madame Oblomov, she does not understand these things. She goes *ka-boomf!*"

"Does she want to see Daniel expelled?"

"Expelled? What is this expelled? Here they make murders but they are not expelled. I mend the car, but Daniel he is underneath with a heavy wrench and he stays there all day."

"How does that appeal to you, Daniel?"

"It's all right."

"You don't seem much concerned."

I wasn't, but I couldn't have said why. I was just living

32

on another planet, far away from Dartington, that was all.

"Daniel," Curry said, sitting up straight, his mind made up, "I have never accepted that there is such a thing as a really bad boy. It is my belief that all children can develop into responsible adults in the end. They respond to reason and trust. Before you mend the car, I want you to do something for me."

I lifted my head.

"There's a child in the junior house who needs to be taken to Exeter for treatment. I would like you to be her escort."

Oh, very smooth, very clever! Put your trust in Daniel, the worst boy in the school, and it will do him good. "Aren't you afraid I'll lose her, or something?" I asked.

"No, Daniel, I am not."

"Who is it, then?"

"A young girl, not English. So far she has not been off the estate by herself, but now she's in need of the dentist. Her name is Esther."

Stupidly, I said, "That's a silly name."

"She is known to you, I believe. . . . No, young man, you must not be tempted to lie. Her housemother has told me of your meeting with Esther yesterday, and the other day Ossi saw you follow her into the wood. She has a meaning for you, I think. I will rely on you to look after Esther as an adult would."

Of course, it was all part of the Dartington *thing*. Trust even an abysmal jellyfish and he will turn into an adult, all in a flash. I knew I'd been edged into a corner.

"Will you do it, Daniel?"

"I'm sure Esther will enjoy your company," Bridget said.

"She hates my guts," I said. "I pushed her in the middle and spoiled her trick. I don't think she'll come with me."

"It has been mentioned to her, and she did not object."

"You've *asked* her?" All at once I was up in the air, at least two feet off the ground.

"We needed to make the arrangements quickly," Curry said. "A car will be provided by the estate."

"It's a lovely drive along the Exeter road," Bridget said.

I asked, "Why not send Bella or Trudi? Why choose a problem child?"

"I have chosen you, Daniel, because I have faith in your intelligence and good nature. I would not entrust the care of a young person to someone I thought unsuitable. Now, will you undertake this task?"

I mooched around Curry's office, looking at this and that.

"Please tell me," Curry said.

"Of course I'll take her," I said, staring into the fireplace.

"And you'll treat her properly?"

"Yes. *Yes.* YES!"

"Very well, Daniel. You will go this afternoon, and to-morrow you will help Ossi to mend the car. You may leave me now."

4

THE CAR THAT TOOK US TO EXETER WAS BLACK
and silent. I'm sure it was expensive, like everything be-
longing to Mrs. Elmhirst. A glass screen separated the
driver from the inside of the car. Esther sat beside me,
looking straight forward and not speaking. Her face was
swollen on the other side. We crossed over the old bridge
at Staverton, where the Dart ran slowly underneath, and
entered the lanes beyond. Here the sunlight lay in pools
along the road.

Esther wore a blue coat with square pockets and a broad
belt which didn't look English. Her black hair was shining
and I wanted to touch it. Once she gave a glance in my
direction but, catching my eye, she looked away again.

I said, "You could've refused to come with me."

"It was, after all, the dentist," she said, meaning that she

35

might as well have all the dreadful things at once.

"They chose me on purpose."

Her eyes flashed in my direction. "Why did they do that?"

"They think it's good for me."

She thought that one over. "Of course, the school is experimental," she said slowly, doubtfully. "They take terrible risks. I shouldn't be surprised if . . ."

"If what?"

She meant that, with me, she might not come back alive.

"It's not very nice being used in an experiment," Esther said. "Why, I might be massacred."

I watched the hedges flying past.

"Massacred," she said. Her face changed suddenly and she was trying not to laugh. "Just think of it! They chose a moron to take me to Exeter."

"I'm not actually a moron. I mean, not all the time."

We were silent then, while the car came out of the lanes and went faster on the main road. Her bottom was rocking from side to side on the soft leather. She expected a compliment.

"Did you mind coming with me today?"

"No," I said. Then, "I was told to come."

The rocking stopped. "You could've said no."

"I could've, but I didn't."

She snorted once or twice.

"Curry arranged it," I said. "It's what he believes in."

"At Dartington, there is always a genius who does things differently." She spoke in her practical voice. "They would not allow it at home."

I said, "Will you tell me where that is?"

"I don't have to tell you anything."

36

She was looking out of the opposite window and I couldn't see her face, only the long hair that cut across her shoulders like a curtain she'd drawn behind her.

"I think you speak German," I said.

"Perhaps I can. Stop asking questions."

"But you're not German."

"No," she said, "of course not! I've lived in this country for some time. My parents are here."

That was obvious, because her English was much better than Trudi's. For a long time we said nothing. She was making small noises which might have been laughter, but in fact the tooth was hurting her.

"I'm not going to cry at the dentist," she said suddenly. "I *won't*."

"I'm sure you won't."

"And you don't have to be nice to me, either. Because they sent you with me, it doesn't mean you have to be nice to me."

Oh, Esther was tough! She didn't care if I liked her or not. She could get on without me. The back of her head was framed in the car window, with the rushing fields beyond.

At the dentist, I sat in the waiting room and looked at old copies of the *Hotspur*—put there, I suppose, for visiting schoolboys. The inner door was open and I could hear the sound of the drill. Occasionally the dentist spoke, but Esther's voice was too low for me to catch. She didn't cry. Once I heard her take a long breath that might have had some blubbing in it, but it was only once. Then she came back into the waiting room, looking rather white.

The dentist came out behind her. "A brave young lady," he said.

She was pleased with that and pleased that I'd heard, and she let me help her with her coat.

We took the coast road back through Starcross and Dawlish. I think the driver had been told to go that way. Esther was less snappy now, and when at Holcombe the driver asked us if we'd like to walk on the beach (God, they were *smart* at Dartington!) she agreed without making a fuss.

We walked under the red cliffs, toward Babbacombe Bay. The driver came onto the beach behind us and stood looking in our direction. A long way ahead I could see Hope's Nose jutting out into the sea, the sunlight falling there, the sea shining. We went to the edge of the water, where we had to dart back with each wave. She laughed when the wave broke over my shoe and I went hopping up the beach.

"You're not quick enough, silly!" Her voice was shrill across the sand.

Farther along, where the cliffs became low, a stream crossed the sand and exposed a line of shingle. We skipped flat stones over the water. Although she tried hard, Esther couldn't throw very well—her wrist wouldn't give the flick she wanted—and usually her stone bounced on the water only once or not at all. I could make a stone skim over a wave and continue out to sea, or I could throw a pebble such a long way you could hardly see the splash.

"You're not bad at throwing," Esther said suddenly.

But she walked backward, putting some space between us, all the same. I sent another pebble a long way out.

"Not that it's much use, throwing things."

Way down the beach the sun was shining. Esther walked to the base of the cliff, where the stream tumbled through a narrow gully, and I followed her. She sat on a rock and drew her knees up to her chin. I stopped two yards away and stood on one foot.

"Why are you standing like that?" She hadn't looked at me, but she knew what I was doing.

"My shoe's full of water."

She looked very pretty, her skirt just covering her knees, her hair hanging loose and dividing at the back to show me a little triangle of white skin.

"Stop looking at me," Esther said.

I turned away.

"Of course, you may not be altogether a moron. There may be something you can do."

"Oh, there *is*," I said.

I kept my eyes upon Hope's Nose, just where it dipped into the sea. From somewhere behind me a gull swooped down, flying exactly toward the point, going a long way before it came down in the water.

"Something not too difficult," said Esther.

There was nothing I *couldn't* do, if I tried. Even Curry had agreed that I was intelligent. I turned back to Esther, and this time she didn't mind. She was holding her skirt down tight over her legs. Her hair was a little black tent enclosing her head and shoulders. She was looking at me with her head lowered, a gleam showing in her eyes, her chin scraping her knees.

The wind was blowing from the point, nudging the clouds, and I saw an edge of sunlight coming along the beach. Then it passed over us and I felt the warmth on the back of my neck. I was going to do something wonderful; that was quite certain. Esther had closed her eyes against the glare—closed them except for a tiny spark that showed under her lids, so that I knew she was still watching me.

"There's a lot I can do," I said, expecting a miracle. "Perhaps."

"I just have to decide what."

She threw back her head, looked up at the sun and said in her low soft voice, "You'd better get on with it, then."

5

I WISH I COULD SAY I WENT TO WORK AFTER
that. In fact, I didn't. You see, I had no idea what I wanted
to be when I was older. Bridget Edwards told me to go
around the studios and workshops, of which there were
a great many at Dartington, and talk to the artists and
craftsmen. Something, she believed, would get me going.
Something like poetry or painting would be just the thing
for me!

I went up to the Hall one morning. The poets were
giving a reading in a corner of the garden. They were men
in baggy coats with too much in their pockets. Their fore-
heads rose through wispy hair. When they read their poetry, they made circular gestures with their arms, and their
arms had too many joints in them. They seemed to be
imitating large pieces of machinery. I sat on the grass while

the poets made noises like the starting of a car or the action of a water pump, but after a while I got tired of it and went away toward the studios where the painters worked.

The painters were different from the poets: they wore boiler suits and berets, and their energy came in short bursts. One painter was dashing at the easel with his head down and occasionally he gave a huge laugh. I watched his picture as it appeared on the canvas: it was of a large ear floating in the clouds with some geometrical shapes at the bottom. I didn't like it much, and neither did he, apparently, because after a while he scraped most of it off and went away in a sulk.

I told Bridget I didn't think much of poetry or painting, and she gave me her worried look. I would have to find an interest in something, she said.

"They all look so silly," I told her.

After that, though I still didn't know where I was going, I went occasionally into Bridget's classroom and sat at the back with Martin and Walter. We threw paper darts when we thought Bridget wasn't looking. Trudi would sometimes get at me for having no ambition, and snort and toss her head in disgust. I didn't mind much because Trudi was disgusted with everybody. And she was *wrong*, as it happens; I did have ambition. I saw myself in a blaze of light, famous. I just didn't know what I was famous *for*.

Of course, there were days when I did nothing, when I just walked in the lanes or watched the animals at the school farm. I was doing that one afternoon, hanging on the fence by the gym, when I caught sight of a patch of blue way up on High Cross Hill. The sun was beating on the hill and the birds were flying around in great circles. I thought it was Esther's coat. The little blue spot was moving slowly, lazily, up toward the beech trees that stood on top of the hill. (I must tell you that, in those summer months, I wasn't too crazy about Esther. I just liked the look of her—how her hair sloshed around like wine in a glass and how her eyes gleamed when she was angry.)

I followed the patch of blue up the lane. At the top of the hill I went through the private gate into the grounds of Dartington Hall, where Mrs. Elmhirst lived. Under the trees there was a glimmer of light, and from high up a swish of leaves in the wind. Mrs. Elmhirst was rich, *rich*; her money came from a great pile in America. The trees were old and tall, but older still was the tiltyard, where years ago the knights had ridden. Now it was a terraced lawn with clipped yews at one end and a screen of trees at the other.

I looked around, hoping to see Esther, but there was nothing but flickering leaf shadow and a fat bee cruising between the bushes. Then I saw a flash of blue down by the lawns and I went snaking after it, only to find it was a clump of lilac and not very blue after all. I stood there listening to the rustle and creak of the garden. A footstep, then something like a voice, and I thought I saw a blue shadow moving away toward the tiltyard. I didn't quite look at it, in case it vanished, and when I did turn my head it was gone, anyway, and I was standing there like a loony, my hands in my pockets, doing nothing.

I sat on a wooden seat near the rose garden, hardly thinking at all. Whoever it had been was gone. (Actually, I never did find out who it was in the blue coat. It may have been Esther, but I'm not sure.) All I know for certain is that, about a minute later, there was a voice beyond my shoulder.

"You are enjoying the garden, young sir?"

The words were soft, American. I turned, to see a tall

woman dressed in gray and wearing a double row of pearls. She was smiling. She was looking over the top of my head, her face on one side, and to tell the truth she looked a bit dotty. She carried an open book which seemed to contain verses.

"I've always said that poetry reads best where there are flowers in bloom," she told me.

I stared, and she didn't look away but bent toward me, her nostrils opening, as if I were some sort of rose. I believed myself to be looking at the richest woman in the world.

I remembered the poets on the lawn, who had seemed such a mess. "Did you write those poems yourself?" I asked.

"Indeed not. The young man who wrote them was here, but he did not stay."

"I see."

"He has gone, I think, to Germany."

She showed me the book: *Poems,* by W. H. Auden. I was still looking at Mrs. Elmhirst, and she just went on nodding and smiling. That *smile.* God, it was big, like a sunrise.

Mrs. Elmhurst took a place beside me on the seat. "You will be a poet, perhaps?"

"I don't think so."

"You will turn to something creative, I am sure."

"How d'you know?"

The smile flashed once to my face before wandering off. She was silent a long time. Then she nodded, as though a message had just come through, and turned to me again. Her voice was so soft I could barely hear it.

"I don't know who you are, young man, but I know you are marked for achievement."

"Do you really think so?" For a moment I saw myself a great *something,* and everybody clapping.

She said "Mmmm . . . ," as if she'd already seen my work, whatever it was, and found it marvelous.

"They don't think much of me at school."

"They don't?"

"I took Madame Oblomov's car to pieces."

"You *did?*"

"I watched the poets and painters at the hall, but they looked rather silly to me. They were just"—I hunted for the word—*"messy."*

Her head went up six inches, as if she'd never thought of it.

"I'll have to do *some*thing," I said.

"Indeed you will!"

"The trouble is, I don't know what I want to be."

She smiled. She knew the answer to that. "It's not a question of what you'll be, young man. It's a question of what you are. *Now.*"

"Now?"

"Of course."

"Oh," I said.

She went into another long "Mmmm . . ." before bringing her hands together and straightening her shoulders. "Now then," she said, "we must find out what it is you like, and no mistake."

She looked away under the trees. She seemed to be listening. All of a sudden I saw her eyes grow round and large, and frankly it was a bit spooky.

"Listen!" she said.

I listened, but there was nothing to hear—nothing but the sound of the trees and a scuttle from the undergrowth, where a bird was poking about.

"What is it?"

"Perhaps there's something for you *there.*"

I giggled, but she wasn't offended.

"Actually, I can't hear anything," I said.

"You can't?"

"Not really."

She looked surprised, as if to say, how could I have missed it? It was *absolutely obvious.* "Well, now. I was almost certain. . . ."

She got up and smoothed down her dress. She didn't look at me directly but as usual at something else, something farther off.

"I would like you to come with me to the Hall," she said. "I would like you to meet a friend of mine."

Together, we walked toward the gray buildings of Dartington Hall. We passed under the high pointed windows and turned into the courtyard. It was all desperately old.

"Who is your friend?" I asked.

"A man involved in the tragedy of Europe," was all she said.

We went through a doorway and climbed a stair. From above I could hear voices speaking in several languages. She took me into a drawing room where a butler was serving tea to a number of guests. Their voices faded when Mrs. Elmhirst came in. She led me to the end of the room, the voices starting up again behind us, where a heavy man with a thick neck and a head shaved like a brush rose stiffly and bowed to Mrs. Elmhirst.

"General Schultz, I want you to meet a young man from the school. It will help him, I think, to talk to you."

He looked at me steadily, at the same time bringing his heels together slowly. "You have a name, huh?"

His English wasn't bad, except for the "huh?" which seemed to belong to another language.

"Daniel," I said.

"The general has been in Spain with the International Brigades," Mrs. Elmhirst said. "He was severely wounded."

I had noticed how the stiffness of his back was due to a metal brace that showed under his coat. This man was held together with screws! It hurt him even to move his eyes.

"The general will be my guest until he is well enough to return to Barcelona." Mrs. Elmhurst said something else—about my difficulty in finding a subject to please me—and at the end of it the general nodded.

"General Schultz has great experience and his advice will be helpful to you," Mrs. Elmhirst said, floating away.

Of help to me? Did she think I'd make a good soldier? Me, the nuisance, the wrecker of cars?

"Tell me about the war in Spain," I said. (I suppose it was cheeky, but we were like that at Dartington.)

"There's little to tell, but that we shall lose it." His voice was cut short by a bout of pain, but he didn't move or say anything. After a time, he went on, "Boys younger than you have already been killed in Spain, huh?"

"Did you command the army?"

General Schultz sat down with a clank of metal. "Forgive me, Daniel. I am unable to stand. No, I commanded some units of the International Brigades. I am not a regular soldier, though I saw service in the German army in the last war."

Even so, I could only think of General Schultz as a soldier. He was so disciplined he made me comb my hair with my fingers.

"Why did you go to Spain?"

Perhaps he thought that funny. He wound his head round, like a gun turret, until he was looking at me.

"My country was supporting the Fascist army. It seemed necessary to redress the balance, no matter in how small a way."

"Was it very exciting?"

"You ask many questions, boy. You take an interest in military things?"

"Not really."

"At Dartington, you do not have soldiers, huh?"

"Oh—*no.*"

"You have a proper regard for liberty."

"I suppose we do. It's a bit of a shambles, though."

He nodded. "You like things, shall I say, well ordered?"

"I don't like a mess." The words spoke themselves and I realized how silly they were. I was one of the messiest children in the school.

"Tell me—I shall not mind if you can give me no answer—would you like to impose an order where at present there seems to be none?"

"I think so."

"That could be the case. Daniel, give me your arm."

I jumped to obey him. I helped him to his feet, hearing the click of metal as some part of the brace locked into the upright position. I couldn't let him go, no matter that I was frightened of his terrible wounds and the metal support. We left the drawing room, waiting a minute so that the general could bow to Mrs. Elmhirst.

"I will take the boy to the great hall. He may find something to interest him there."

We took ten minutes to reach the hall, which wasn't far. With each step I could feel the pain running through his body.

"What are they doing in the hall?" I asked.

"You will see. They impose an order, perhaps. They make sense of the absurd."

"What does that mean?"

"Wait, Daniel! You have time enough to find out."

We entered the great hall, where our footsteps echoed under the beamed roof. Patches of sunlight lay under the tall windows. There was a low stage at one end of the hall, and here a small orchestra was seated, their instruments put down. I'd seen the same sort of thing often enough on the estate.

"It's only an orchestra," I said.

"As you say, boy. It is only an orchestra."

When they caught sight of the general, the musicians rose to their feet, surprising me, for we didn't do things like that at Dartington.

"Why are they standing? Is it because you're a general?"

"I think not."

"Will they play?"

All at once he grew tired! "Yes, they will play. They can do nothing else. Daniel, I wish you to hear the Baroque Ensemble of Spain, whom Mrs. Elmhirst has been pleased to welcome to her home because, at present, they have nowhere to go. Now take this chair and be silent. Gentlemen, the Minuet and Badinerie."

In fact, I'd heard the Bach suite before. We played it sometimes on a large-horned gramophone in the music room. And I remembered parts of it from the choir school, where we'd had a class called "musical appreciation," or something. Now, for once, I listened. I couldn't do anything else because General Schultz had bent forward, his chin on his knuckles, his eyes closed. His concentration was so great I thought his head would split open.

49

The music was exact, lively, and not too long.

When the piece was finished, the general kept his eyes on the floor. I'd expected him to speak to the musicians but instead he turned to me.

"Music, Daniel. In music there can be no mess. There can be no misunderstanding, no pretense, only an exquisite order. Did you like the piece?"

I thought about it. I had enjoyed the tidiness of the music and the skill of the playing. Beyond that, I hadn't felt much. "I liked it better than I did at choir school," I said.

"Choir school? What is this about a choir school?"

"I went to one until I was ten. I can read music a little."

"So? You have sung the great works?" His eyes bulged at me. "Then, then . . ."

"What?" I asked.

"Then the lady may not have been mistaken. I had thought it her fantasy." He was speaking to himself, but then he faced me again. "Well, boy, you have heard the best that men can do in a tormented world. Can you match them?"

"I'm not sure," I said.

"Can you make peace with the unknowable? Can you accept a discipline as harsh as any soldier's forgetting Dartington and its freedoms?"

"I would like to do something really difficult," I told him, and he raised his head as if I'd said something important. "You see, I tried to take a car through a window, because it was difficult and no one had done it before."

"You did that?"

"I watched the poets and painters, but their work seemed too easy."

He looked at me for a long time, before saying, mostly

to himself, "I've seen worse. Many worse. Perhaps it's just possible. . . ."

"Do you think—" I began.

"I think nothing, boy. I have only an impression. But I think you will do best within a precise discipline. Dartington has not offered you a sufficient challenge, so you take a car through a window. I will think about it and perhaps send a friend of mine to help you."

When we returned to the drawing room, Mrs. Elmhirst came up, the smile very bright, and asked me to sit next to her. "You enjoyed the music, young sir?"

I said, "Yes."

"You know, of course, that Joachim Schultz is one of the finest composers in Europe?"

"I thought he was a general."

She took no notice of *that,* which was kind. "May I hope that we have helped you this afternoon?" she asked.

It would have been rude to say no, so I said yes instead.

Mrs. Elmhirst touched my hand lightly, nodded more than once, and made the contented sound she'd made earlier:

"*Mmmm. . . .*"

In the next week, while it grew toward summer, I went each day to see General Schultz at the Hall. I was a bit frightened of him, particularly when he stared at me without speaking and made huffing noises. He tested my knowledge of music and gave me short pieces to read and describe. It was odd to find how much I could remember from my years at choir school. I did exactly what he told me—can you believe it?—and I wasn't late once. I even washed my hands and cleaned my fingernails. Bridget tried not to show how surprised she was, but once I saw her lift her hands in a little flurry of excitement and skip a couple of paces, to which, of course, I paid no attention.

General Schultz had promised to send someone to help me—and he did! Professor Bolski came down to Foxhole on a bicycle, tilting left and right like a shambling old horse. He was a small man with moist eyes and a habit of blowing his nose whether he needed to or not. He was, so he told me, a Jewish refugee; he'd been helped out of Germany by Mrs. Elmhirst and now had a job at the music school. One day I asked him why he'd been chosen as my instructor. He pulled at his chin and hooked his feet together under the music stool.

"I have some reputation as a teacher of composition," he said modestly, "and Joachim Schultz has advised Mr. Curry that your gift may lie in that field."

"Gosh," I said. (Daniel, the great composer!)

"You will have to work hard, with strict discipline. You will have little time for leisure."

I said nothing.

"Schultz believes you can do it. You have an anarchic mind governed by a sense of order."

"I have?" I thought about Schultz and his metal waistcoat. "D'you know that Schultz was blown up by a grenade and lost most of his guts but went on fighting?"

"That is so, Daniel."

"What a thing to happen when you're leading an army!"

But Professor Bolski didn't know about armies.

"I think I can do it," I said. "I don't mind how strict it is. Gosh! Old Schultz. . . ."

"He would have taught you himself—"

"Why? He'd never seen me before."

"He felt, I think, the need to put a new student to work

52

before returning to Spain. I cannot tell you his motives precisely."

I was impatient at first, hoping to learn it all at once, getting angry at what seemed to be a subject without an end. And meanwhile it was summer outside, and the dragonflies were playing over the Dart, up and down the river, and it was hard to separate them from the flashing of the stream.

6

SUMMER, SUMMER. IT WAS WARM, AND ANY-
thing seemed possible. Now we sat in the courtyard in
untidy groups. Sometimes Esther was there, and she would
give me a sideways look, but she never said anything. In
fact, the first time we spoke was at the midsummer holiday,
when the sun was blazing on the courtyard walls and I saw
her in the covered passageway by the assembly hall. Everywhere there were children whose voices came and went like
puffs of wind.

Esther wasn't doing anything, just standing in shadow
and staring at the ground. I had to walk all around her and
duck down, bringing myself exactly in front of her eyes,
before she admitted that Daniel the delinquent was *any-
where at all.* Then she shook her head to get rid of the awful
sight.

"They tell me you've gone all musical," she said. "What a thought!"

"There was this man, this general—" I began.

"It was time you did something."

She stepped into the courtyard, into the sunlight, and moved away, but she went so slowly I knew I was meant to follow—and I did, of course. (She was leading me by the nose, and not for the last time, either!) After three steps she stopped and turned halfway toward me. Under her lashes her eyes swung until they were watching me.

"Bet you don't go on with it."

"Bet you I do."

From the other side of the courtyard Bella was looking toward us, rather obviously. She had a small mirror in her hand, which she'd been using to reflect the sun round the walls, and now she turned it until the light fell on Esther's face.

"Got you!" she said, from way over there.

I can tell you that Esther didn't mind too much; she smiled in the fierce white light as if she enjoyed the attention. She moved her head about, playing with the beam. My eyes were fixed on her face, which had turned pale. I wanted to run my finger down her nose, and then the other way along her lips, but of course I didn't do either of those things. I just stood there, like a booby.

"She's too young for you, Daniel," Bella shouted. "She's got no tits."

God, Bella could be crude sometimes! (Actually, Bella had tits that were quite good when she had them fastened up, and her middle wasn't too bad either, if she held her belly in. And she moved with a sort of ripple. But I wasn't going to look at her now.)

"Don't bother about Bella," I said.

I could have saved my breath because Esther had paid no attention, anyway. Her eyes were gleaming. She was living in a different place from Bella and me, somewhere superior, and I was no more important than an ant. When Bella turned the beam away, Esther gave a small shrug, ground her shoe on the paving stone (crushing the ant, presumably) and went back into the shade of the covered way.

"We could go walking, as we did on the beach," I said eagerly. I had the crazy notion she might come down to the river.

"I'm going out with the others," Esther said, turning away, her skirt sweeping round behind her like a slamming door.

"Where?"

"Nowhere."

I was angry with Esther for giving herself airs. I hadn't done anything to upset her recently. I stood looking at the door where she had disappeared and where, I was sure, the air was still quivering.

Damn Esther. I moved off along the courtyard wall, glaring into windows. Of course, she was too thin to be any good to anyone. She might break into pieces. And it was certainly true that she had no tits. I stamped round the courtyard, going nowhere in particular, until I fell over Bella. She looked at me through dusty eyes, which the sun had nearly closed. She braced her shoulders so that her bust lifted inside her shirt, and as the shirt was open at the neck I could see down into the shadowy place where her tits were like two oranges pressed together and flattened in the middle. Bella wouldn't come to pieces. Her clothes had opened at the waist and her bellybutton was showing. She was flapping the tail of her shirt to keep cool. She looked like a burst parcel.

She got up. She'd been waiting for me to fall over her, almost certainly. (I had better make it clear that I'd never thought much of Bella, who just about everybody had messed about with, but just then the sun was lying in the fields around Foxhole and I felt like doing something different—something secret and daring and which had a lot to do with Bella's shirt being open at the front.)

"Bella," I said, "I'm going down to the river. You could come, if you wanted."

She looked surprised, but she started swinging her bottom, all the same.

We climbed the hill to High Cross, feeling the warmth. Bella walked ahead of me, in a hurry to get to the river, her bottom rolling under a skirt that was too small for her and had a hole in it. Of us all, Bella had grown the most, and now she was bigger than I was. Along the other side of the hedge, so that we could see her now and again, came Trudi, in a purple dress.

"I thought you'd got stuck with music." Bella spoke crossly, going faster. "I mean, the summer will be over soon. What's Trudi doing?"

"Watching, I think."

"How did she know?"

"Know what?"

I was dragging my feet a little. It dawned upon me that this was a mistake. I wanted to go back to the music room at Foxhole, which had double doors you could fasten on the inside. We went into the Hall garden, where it was warm and shadowy under the trees, like being a long way beneath the sea.

"Trudi's just envious," Bella said. "Her legs are too thick at the bottom."

Bella didn't look at her own legs but I saw the muscles tighten at the thighs. Now she was teetering from one side of the path to the other, losing her balance, ready to fall into the flowerbeds. She was stroking her hips, pretending to slide her bloomers off. She was all wound up and about to explode. I heard the gate slam a long way behind us as Trudi came into the garden.

My cheeks felt hot. My ears buzzed a little. I was being marched toward something I no longer wanted and I counted my footsteps: one, two, three . . .

"Come *on*," Bella said, more than once.

I looked up at the blue sky above the branches, where there was nothing but a blue haze. I wondered if it could change into a crashing storm, lightning cutting down between the trees and a torrent of rain sending us back to Foxhole. But the sun kept shining through the leaves, the heat rising from the path.

I stopped, and Bella looked back impatiently. There were people on the terraced lawns below us. People moving gracefully and speaking English and French. The members of the dance school were warming up on the grass, leaping about like startled goats. Perhaps there were sixteen, and they were nearly naked. For a time we watched them from behind a shrub, Bella tittering, my ears becoming more noisy. The ballet master was hidden under the nearest terrace, but I could hear his voice and the clap of his hands, which, all at once, sent the dancers to an arranged position.

"Dancing's lovely," Bella said.

"Yes."

"I shall be a dancer. . . ."

58

She was much too clumsy, as it happened, but I didn't say so. Then, at another clap, the dancers made slow movements, forming couples, changing, while somewhere a piano played.

"Exciting isn't it?" Bella said.

Actually, it was just sexy.

"I suppose so. Shall we go?"

They were swaying like plants in the wind and I wished they would stop. I wanted them to go away altogether. I spoke inside my head, saying, "Make them go *away.*"

Then they were lying on the grass, and one was climbing on to another, until there was this great heap of flesh in the middle of the lawn.

"*Ahhh!*" said Bella, which sounded like a puncture.

I looked away, and by chance I saw someone moving down by the clipped hedges at the end of the lawn. It was a boy in a white shirt, who was tugging an odd-looking cart along the far side of the hedge, where the dancers couldn't see him. Martin, up to something. Walter was at the rear of the cart, pushing, and it was clear that the cart was heavy and inclined to turn over. I saw a solid platform mounted on baby-carriage wheels, which supported two upright pillars between which a long arm was balanced. Above the base of the arm a weight could be lifted by a block and tackle; the opposite end was a cup-shaped container. A catapult, of course.

"Stop!" Martin whispered.

"Left a little. . . ."

"*Too much!*"

"It's Martin," I told Bella. "He's brought a slingshot. Isn't that funny?"

"But he'll spoil the dancing. How rotten of him!"

I laughed, then. *Good old Martin!*

Walter produced a large balloon, which he carried with both hands underneath it. Its sluggish ripple told me it was full of water. He put it in the container at the far end of the arm. The raising of the weight, which would fall on the pad at the other end, took a lot of doing. Then Martin, the great engineer, stood with his hands on the release lever while the heap of bodies was still sliding about on the lawn.

"*Bravo! C'est magnifique!*" said the ballet master.

The weight fell, the balloon went up in a long climb over the grass—up, up in the direction of the dancers.

"*Pour finir, avec le plus de sentiment. . . .*"

But the balloon was too weak to stand the strain, and when it began to come down, the rubber burst open, making a *pop* I could just hear and scattering water in the air. Martin never got things completely right.

"Oh dear," said an English voice, "the rain! How very tiresome."

They sprang up from the grass and ran under the trees, saying what a pity it was. The ballet master shot like a bullet from his place under the bank.

I got up from behind the bush. "They won't come back," I said. "Not for a long time."

We went on in the direction of the river. At last we came to a field that ran down to the Dart and I saw a flash of water a long way below us. Halfway down the hill, where it was spotted with small flowers, sat Trudi, facing away from us.

We stopped when we reached her. I said, "Hello Trudi."

Her head swung back and forth, in a mood.

"We're just going down the river."

She didn't speak and the bees buzzing around the clover made the only sound.

60

"Come on," said Bella. "Trudi isn't coming."

Now Trudi was humming like a top. Finally she said, her shoulders rocking, "Don't you realize that you can get *diseases?*"

"She's just being silly," Bella said.

"Silly," I said.

"Well—what diseases?"

Trudi gave a short laugh and closed her mouth with a snap. She came from Germany, where they knew about diseases.

"Let's go," said Bella, starting down the hill.

"In some countries there are laws," Trudi went on, raising her voice.

Bella spoke over her shoulder. "So what? It's different at Dartington."

"Laws! Laws!"

Trudi threw herself into the grass, away from us, and started to cry.

"She's jealous," Bella said, skipping down the hill toward the river.

I followed slowly. From the bottom of the slope Trudi was just a splodge of purple a long way above us. We went through a gate and onto a long stretch of grass beside the river, which we called the Marsh. Farther down, and shimmering in the haze, was Folly Island. It wasn't really an island, only a clump of trees facing the river, with a ditch behind it, but it had a grassy bank from which you could jump into deep water and it was here we often came to bathe. We crossed the ditch and went on to Folly Island.

"There are children at the pool," I said.

Between the trees I could see the white bodies of naked children as they leaped into the Dart. They were shining with water and their excited voices carried to where we stood.

"Damn," said Bella, chewing a grass stem.

"They may stay all morning. They do, often. They may have brought lunch."

"We'll sit here until they go."

Bella found a hollow that was damp smelling and filled with rushes and ferns. When she lay in this she was below the level of the path. I followed, slowly.

It was Bella who spoke first. "Well . . . ," she said.

"They say," I began, "—I don't know if it's true, of course—that you can start too soon. I mean . . ."

She reclined beside me, huge, *and actually alive.* Her breath played over me like a damp washcloth. "They say all sorts of things," she said.

"You can have a nervous breakdown."

"Watch me."

"Or fits."

(Trudi had bothered me, of course.)

Now Bella raised herself on her elbow and looked at me. Her large brown eyes ran over my face to see if I was serious. Then she said, "I don't believe it."

"There was a boy at Haileybury. He broke out in patches."

"Really?"

"I remember."

"This is Dartington. Not Haileybury."

The voices were loud at the river and I dropped my head below the level of the ground. I didn't want anybody to see us there. Bella's unblinking eyes were close to mine. I had to do something, so I put my arm round her, feeling the tightness of her shirt, and drew her shoulders toward me

62

until she became blurred and her breath made a storming noise in my ear.

I said. "Perhaps it doesn't matter, this being Dartington. . . ."

She held her lips still, one inch from mine. The cries of the children at the pool were farther off. Almost gone. When my lips, just for a moment, bashed against hers, I found them wet and tasting of grass, and I pulled away from her.

"What are you waiting for?" Bella asked.

In fact, I was waiting for something more to happen, something new and surprising, like a shooting star, but just then I felt only the heavy nearness of Bella's body and how the dampness was getting into my clothing at the elbow and hip.

I put my lips somewhere on the upper part of her body and she rocked like a boat.

"Lovely," she said.

"Lovely," I replied.

"Silly old Trudi. . . ."

Down by the river the sun was shining on the water and sparks of light were flashing over the trees. I heard a grown-up voice calling the children out of the water, and raising my head I saw them climbing the bank and running for their towels. They looked very happy.

Five minutes later they were passing us, behind the trees, making for the Marsh and Foxhole, and it was then that I realized which children they were. How stupid of me not to have guessed! They were shouting and laughing and they looked to be blown along by the wind.

Leading the others was a dark girl whose hair streamed out behind her. Esther, of course. She ran so fast the others could not catch her. She twisted through the trees, making her lead even greater. She seemed to float, missing the trees by some sort of miracle. It looked as if the trees bent away from her, letting her pass. She glanced at the children crashing along behind her and I saw her smile. Then she was gone beyond the wood and on to the Marsh, where her figure became edged with sunlight. The others followed in a clumsy group, shouting, telling her to wait.

Bella poked me in the side. "Wake up," she said.

"It wasn't anything."

"You were miles away." Now she was going to be offended. "There's something about that girl that upsets you."

I looked down the Marsh but Esther's figure had got mixed up with the others. Then they vanished at the end of the field and the sun blazed on the empty grass.

We looked through the trees toward Folly Pool, where the water was now still, and Bella said, "Well, let's go!"

We got up from the crushed ferns and crossed slowly to the river. Here the grass bank hung over the cool, bracken-colored water. Upstream the Dart disappeared into the woods; below us the surface was broken where the river widened and ran over pebbles. We undressed where we stood, without saying anything, leaving our clothes on the grass.

Of course, I'd seen all the girls without their clothes on, because at Dartington no one wore a bathing suit, but now, hidden in the trees, with Bella standing naked beside me, I tried not to look at her. She was a great white slug. For a moment we stood on the edge of the river. My eyes darted to her body and I saw how the tan ended halfway up her thighs. Her belly was pale, like a rumpled sheet, and her breasts lolled this way and that.

"I can swim underwater," she said, plunging in.

She made a great hole in the river, a wave breaking on either side. She swam away from me, but she wasn't actually under the surface because her bottom kept breaking out, making a splash. In the middle of the river she rose and turned toward me, her hair covering most of her face.

"Did you see?"

"Yes."

"Come on, then."

I stepped into the river and swam slowly toward her. She flipped water into my face. "We'll swim upstream," I said.

She leaped on my back, bringing most of the river as well, and I felt her breasts sliding over me. I felt myself sinking under her soft weight until I was peering into the brown, murky depths of the river, smothered by the water as I might have been by a tangle of bedclothes. Down and down I went. I was trapped and frightened. I struggled free and came back to the surface.

"What's the matter, Daniel? Don't you want to play?"

"I was getting my breath."

"I don't think you like sex really."

"It's all right."

Bella was treading water a yard away, like a dolphin standing on its tail. "That girl. She spoiled it all."

"I don't know what you mean," I said.

But she swam away from me—four angry strokes—took a deep breath, and disappeared. I waited for her to come up again. She broke the water just where I knew she would.

"You're just dotty about Esther. I can't think why. She's got no figure at all."

"It's not like that," I said.

But Bella wasn't listening. She was swimming for the bank, with enormous strokes, and I saw her climb out in a great surge of feathery water.

7

AS FAR AS I WAS CONCERNED, AFTER SHE RAN through the wood, Esther went running on forever, because I didn't see her again *for six months*. She just vanished, dissolved into the air. (I may as well tell you that Esther made a habit of disappearing in a flash of light, without a word, until finally she went away altogether.) Bridget told me later that her parents had taken her to Europe for the rest of the summer, even though the term wasn't over yet.

I went on with music, in some sort of temper, and I think Professer Bolski was startled. I think he was even a little frightened. When we met each afternoon he opened his eyes a fraction wider and his head made dodging movements. Now he was showing me how the notes and chords related to one another, how key changes could alter the mood from happy to sad. As the term drew to an end, he continued our classes into the evenings. Sometimes he just played at the piano, music I hadn't heard. Sometimes he forgot that I was there and went bashing on through a long piece. But in the end he always came back to earth with a jolt, saying, "Enough! I do not know why I play such things. The old Europe is forgotten now—forgotten!"

I knew that Bolski was a Polish Jew who had lived for many years in Germany, teaching composition at the University of Leipzig, but I didn't know much else about him.

One afternoon he was really upset. He was listening to my exercises, but his hands were making fluttering movements, rising and falling on their own. We were studying simple modulations at the piano, and I was getting as rattled as he was, though I didn't know why.

"Is someome coming?" I asked.

"Yes, someone is coming. And that it distresses me need not concern you—nor anyone else in the world!" Then a minute later, "Daniel, forgive me! Today I am not myself. You now invert the theme in the relative minor, please."

At last there was a knock at the door and the professor jumped up, losing his spectacles. Mrs. Elmhirst came in, on tiptoe, going sideways. She was followed by General Schultz, walking with a stick. The professor bowed more than once.

"Professor—we are *sorry.*" Mrs. Elmhirst gave the word a lot of drama that seeemed unnecessary. "As you know, we have little time."

"As I know," Bolski said.

"The general's train leaves in half an hour."

The general had nothing to say. He stood upright and his face didn't even twitch. But then he slowly raised one hand, turning the palm upward and opening the fingers. He was letting something fly away, something like a bird.

I think the professor nodded or gave some sign that he understood. Then, surprising me, the two men hugged each other and I heard the clash of metal. I sat with one finger on the keyboard, waiting for them to go. Finally Mrs. Elmhirst put her hand under the general's arm and helped him away, and I saw how his steps were taken stiffly—so stiffly he looked like a toy soldier—and how he bumped into the door as he went out.

The professor went from window to window, straightening the curtains. "What could I do?" he said later. "Nothing! I have influence no longer."

I said, without thinking about it, "Old Schultz is going back to Spain."

"Once I had authority. Once I would have said, This is madness, you do not go! A great composer does not throw his life away. And he would have obeyed me. You see, he was my pupil."

"I didn't know that."

"My most gifted pupil. He is with me seven years in Leipzig. But, Daniel, there comes a time when master and pupil change their places. Always it is so! Then the former master must admit his subservience and say nothing. One day, perhaps . . ."

"Yes?"

"It does not mater now. We continue, please."

We went on for some minutes but his mind wasn't on it. "Joachim Schultz believes you can go far in music," he said. "He leaves you in my charge."

I said nothing to that.

"Perhaps he is right. Perhaps not. You have made good progress."

I said, "I would like to compose."

Suddenly he was thrashing about in all directions like a

tree in a breeze. "*Of course* you will compose! In the generosity of nature there is always a replacement—sometimes better, sometimes not. It is a law! But, believe me, you will need God's utmost favor to be better than Joachim Schultz."

He bounced around on the stool for a bit. Then he settled down and blew his nose noisily. "Now then, Daniel. Attend to me again. . . ."

It was no different in the autumn. We went on bashing the piano. Now there were new faces at Foxhole, among them children from America who wore white caps, sweaters with numbers on the back and rolled-down socks. They had different voices and different bicycles. The most obvious of these were Royden Clancy and his sister Marcelline, from California. They were tall, smart and very polite.

The freedom we had at Dartington, which we didn't think about much, gave Royden quite a shock. He rocked about on his heels, asking, "It is true, you can do just *anything?* Well, that is truly something!"

Esther wasn't there. Her room on the ground floor stayed locked, with the curtains drawn. She was in Europe, they said, where her father was "resisting oppression," and she might not return until the winter. I got into a mood about that and went storming down to the farm and glared at the pigs. But in fact I had only a vague memory of Esther's face at that time and there were moments when I couldn't see her at all. I saw her best as she had been at Holcombe Sands, sitting on the rock, her eyes nearly closed but with a light inside them, but that was way back in the spring.

The autumn was warm, without rain. It was still possible to walk in the woods, where the yellowing light made patterns under the trees. Here, too, you could see rotting wood colored orange and scarlet and brown. Sometimes Trudi came with me and I didn't send her away. (We'd all become nicer to Trudi, whose father, we were told, was being "persecuted by the Nazis" in Germany.) With me, she became timid, no longer full of rages, and anxious to agree. Occasionally she spoke about the need for world revolution, but that was just for show, I think. She smiled when I spoke to her and made no fuss about anything. For the time being, Trudi was behaving in a very refined way and everyone was amazed. (It didn't last, of course.)

The warm days went on into October. In the barn at Shinners Bridge they were storing apples for the cider press and the smell was all over the lane. A mist rose to blur the wood and to hang over the fields. Then the wind came, driving away the smell of apples and sending the clouds racing over High Cross Hill.

Now Trudi took the place next to mine in Bridget's classroom. (I'd better tell you that Bella had moved away as far as she could get after our visit to Folly Island, and she was now a bit dazzled by Royden Clancy in his white cap.) I was embarrassed by Trudi. She would bring her desk closer to mine with tiny shoves until they were touching. I don't think Bridget noticed, but often there was a snigger from the back (Martin, probably) and a voice you could just hear singing "Love is the Sweetest Thing." Classes were usually noisy, so it made no difference.

Then the winter came, with frost all over the fields and ice spreading along the edges of the Bidwell. When we returned to Foxhole in January, after the holiday, the sky was thick and soon the snow fell. At first there was barely enough to cover the ground outside the music room, but then it came down quickly, filling in footprints as soon as they were made.

Still Esther wasn't there. She was somewhere else, lost. . . .

On the first day of the snow, I found Professor Bolski already sitting at the piano when I went for my music lesson. He didn't look up. He was playing a piece I had never heard, something dark and tense and full of strange harmonies. German, of course. He said, without breaking off, "You will not know this piece, Daniel. It is beautiful music. It was brought to me by a student one dull day in Leipzig and it has stayed in my mind ever since."

He was edgy, and his back was stiff. He ended the piece and then without warning struck four violent chords that had nothing to do with it. "So, this is Daniel, who comes for his music lesson!"

"Is something wrong?"

"Nothing."

"What shall I do?"

"Do? You will sit at the piano and play without preparation. You will play me a piece at least as good as the one you've just heard—without fault, without correction."

"You know I can't do that."

"Why not, pray?"

I was getting tired of his mood. I wandered around the room, kicking the furniture. "It was Schultz's music, wasn't it?"

"Yes."

"And I suppose he wrote it when he was twelve, or something."

"He was seventeen."

I went to the window farthest from the piano, where the snow was banked against the panes. I remembered how

Schultz had come into the music room, how he had raised a hand to let something fly, and how he had banged into the door as he went out.

"He's dead, isn't he."

The professor turned sharply to the keyboard and played something without touching the notes. "There is a place called Teruel. I do not know where it is—somewhere, I believe, in the east of Spain. It is the aim of the Spanish government to hold it against the Fascists for military reasons I cannot follow. It was there, three days ago, that the Fifteenth International Brigade went into action against the rebels."

I ran my finger along the snow's edge. Outside, a long way off, I could see the figures of children, bright against the snow.

"They claim to have killed many Fascists. But always they will say many were killed when they must admit their own bitter defeat. About midday, Daniel, somewhere outside the town, the general was struck."

"Yes?"

His mind had drifted off. His fingers played another series of notes, this time on the lid of the piano. "How was it, do you think, that a disabled man could be allowed so close to the fighting? Also I find it repellent that a man held together by metal . . ."

I blew on the windowpane, making a dull spot where I could draw with my finger. I drew a circle, then canceled it out.

"He lay there, still living, while the loyalists retreated toward Teruel. They were unable to reach him with medical aid. Finally, from high ground north of the town, the loyalists watched the Fascists advance down the valley and reach the general. There was nothing they could do." He

73

gave an absurd little laugh. "There was nothing they could do, Daniel, not even when they saw the general tied to a tree—tied with many bindings, because he could not stand—to be shot through and through by the Fascist riflemen."

"Is that what happened?"

"Through and through, through and through. . . ."

"Oh."

At once the professor tidied his clothes and ran his fingers through his hair. He stood up to straighten his trousers.

"Very well, Daniel. That is the truth of the new Europe. We think no more about it. Come now, I will hear your exercises. . . ."

The snow fell again that evening. After supper I went into the assembly hall, where they were dancing. I sat on the edge of the stage and watched as the couples went round and round. Only Royden and Marcelline Clancy danced really well, with lots of spurts and flourishes; the rest just shuffled round the floor while the gramophone played "Little Old Lady" and "Small Hotel."

Someone was watching me. It was like a beam of light. But when I raised my eyes I saw just the dancers and a group of children romping around near the gramophone. Whoever it was had gone. I forgot it then and drummed my heels against the stage in time with the music. Shuffle, shuffle, shuffle, the dancers went. Minutes later I was being watched from another part of the room and this time I didn't look up. I hadn't the courage. My heart began to thump. I just kept my eyes on the revolving dancers until I knew the watcher had left by the open door, going out into the snow.

I had to do something, so I danced with Bella, pushing her around the edge of the floor, making a turn at each corner. She was glum as hell, and she kept looking over my shoulder at something a long way off.

After a bit, she said, "You don't dance very well, do you?"

"No."

"I'd've thought you would've, with all that music."

We collided with Royden and Marcelline, who were dashing across the floor with a lot of tiny steps.

"For heaven's sake," said Bella. "Whatever's the matter with you?"

"They got in the way."

We made another circuit of the floor, barging into couples here and there. I said, "Old Schultz . . ."

"What about him? Look, must you go the same way around? It's possible to *reverse,* you know. What about Schultz?"

"He was in Spain."

"So's everyone else."

"At a place called Teruel. . . ."

This time we hit Royden and Marcelline quite hard, just when they were teetering backward. They went over in a great sprawl of arms and legs, and everybody stopped dancing to look.

"Now see what you've done." Bella was angry now, and embarrassed. I think she was in love with Royden in his ridiculous white cap. "And just when they were dancing so beautifully!"

"They're not hurt. Not really."

The music had stopped and I went to the wall. I had expected Bella to walk away with Royden but instead she came back to me. She'd got something else to say.

75

"Of course, you're too small to dance properly. I like it best with someone taller than me. And you could brush your hair."

"All right," I said.

I went out by the terrace door to where the snow lay thick and the cold was brimming. Over the fields a moon had risen. Behind me the music still played.

I followed the drive toward the gate until the sound faded out and my ears rang with the silence and cold. The moon was sailing above the trees, clear and very large.

A snowball flew past my ear and I turned sharply. Nothing there. Nothing but the banks of snow under the moon and, farther back, the windows of Foxhole all alight. Some moron in the trees, probably. I went on to the gate, and there I stood, a sitting target, wondering which way to turn.

This time the snowball went skying over my head to break a long way down the lane. I ducked under the hedge, into shadow, and I stayed there listening. It was a rotten shot, actually. Someone who couldn't throw. Slowly I raised my head above the level of the hedge and looked into the dark, but I saw no one. I waited, peering forward, looking at the moonshadows—like an absolute fool, of course.

The next one got me right in the face. *Splat!*

A figure, small, like a blown leaf, darted from one snowdrift to another. I ran to the place where the figure had disappeared, but still I couldn't see anyone. Then, on my left and far away, there was a laugh—rather superior—and I knew that I was still watched.

How stupid I must have looked, charging through the snow in the wrong direction. What a jellyfish! I slipped behind a tree and waited. Then from the corner of my eye

I saw a shadow sliding over the dark ground near the lane, but when I turned it was gone.

"You look silly, standing there!"

A low voice, speaking quietly, which came from nearby. I made a snowball and sent it whizzing in that direction, but I heard it break in the frosted leaves.

"Missed," the voice said.

"You think you're very clever."

"Cleverer than you."

I made a dash toward the voice, plowing like a bullock through a drift, and this time I brought the snowballer up against a tree. The black head drove into my chest, but I kept my arms on either side of the small, quivering body, holding it firmly against the tree.

"I thought it was you," I said.

Esther's face turned sharply upward. It was some sort of challenge. Her features were blurred, but I saw the shining eyes and the small round mouth. Dull shadows ran over her face as she pulled backward and forward. The hair that lay over my hand was soft and flashing in the moonlight.

"Why did you follow me?" I asked.

"You looked so gloomy in the hall."

Still I hadn't let her go. I watched her face, which had grown older. Her forehead was below the level of my eyes, showing me that I was still taller. Just.

"You looked terrible, like a ghost," Esther said, rubbing it in.

I let her go, slowly, but I kept one wrist in my hand. "Why weren't you here last term?" I asked.

"I was abroad with my parents. In Europe."

"What was it like in Europe?"

"There were banners everywhere."

"What for?"

She snorted, meaning I should have known. "They were celebrating the Nazi party."

Her wrist was so thin my fingers met on the far side. If I let her go, she would, I thought, rush into the trees. We made our way down the lane, step by step, toward a place where a stone stairway led up to the clock tower. At the bottom of the stairs she turned her wrist quickly, violently, breaking my hold, but though she looked into my face with a flash of temper she didn't run away.

"Pax altogether," she said.

I went up the stairs and she followed three steps behind. Once, I turned toward her and she ran down again, but only to stop and come slowly back when I didn't chase after her. Finally we reached the top more or less together and went into the forecourt. A low wall surrounded the terrace and here I sat in the stinging cold while she stayed a yard off, facing away from me.

"You'd better go in," I said. "It's cold."

She came toward me, walking sideways, in a shaky movement I can still remember. (*O God, I can remember it!*) Her face was pale, the same color as the moon, the eyes large, the lips just open.

She said, "What happened today? To you, I mean. Gosh, you looked *awful.*"

"Nothing much."

"I thought you'd been expelled or something."

"No."

"Someone must have died, *at least.*"

"Yes."

"They did. Who?"

Her elbow had drifted too close, and now I grabbed it and pulled her onto my lap in a bundle. I pinned her arms

78

to her sides, buried my face in her back, and rubbed my cheek up and down against her raincoat.

"Old Schultz," I said. *"Old Schultz."*

Then I thumped her three times with my chin. She struggled free and backed away, her eyes furious.

"You said you wouldn't do that."

"I know."

She kicked the snow in my direction. "I knew you'd break your word."

"Yes."

"Who's Old Schultz, then?"

"A man I met at the Hall. A man who said I could do music."

"You mean, he just died."

"They shot him, tied to a tree."

"Oh." She turned a complete circle, drilling a hole in the snow with her heel. "In Europe, I suppose."

"It was in Spain."

"Just now you grabbed me. Why'd you do that?"

"I felt like it."

She came closer, examining my face. She said, making each word enormous, "YOU—MUST—BE—A—MON-STER—AT—LEAST."

"I suppose so."

"I'd better go in."

"No!"

I reached for her hand, violently, but stopped before I touched her. She snatched her arm away but stayed where she was, breathing heavily.

"Gosh, what's it all about? This Schultz. . . ."

I had a picture of him in my mind, not tied to the tree, but as he'd been in the music room when he came to say good-bye. "I didn't know him well," I said. "He was very strict and didn't smile much, but he made me work. He showed me that I could learn music. Why did he bother?" Her dark eyes jumped to my face, suddenly puzzled. "And now . . . ," I went on.

"And now," she said in her important voice, "you'll have to go on. You'll have to be brilliant. There's nothing else you can do."

I hadn't seen it like that, but Esther had come from Europe just the other day, and in Europe they understood these things better than we did. They were *serious*. They sat in rows.

"I suppose so," I said.

She took a step toward me, not frowning, but with her eyes rather intense and her cheeks drawn into hollows.

The next bit I can remember more clearly than anything else. She swung her hand toward my face and I did nothing to stop it. Her fingers brushed my cheek, not too gently. Then she did the same on the other side. She ended up by pushing my nose with her thumb, as she might have pushed a starting button. I didn't know if I'd been stroked or just hit, and I don't think Esther knew, either.

The music was reaching us from the assembly hall, where the others were still dancing. It was a long way off, in another world. I wanted to grab her again, but I didn't do it. We just stayed where we were in the tingling cold, no more than an arm's length apart, looking at each other, saying nothing.

8

WHEN THE SNOW VANISHED, THE WIND CAME back, driving the rain against the classroom windows. To my surprise I was elected to the school council for this new year of 1938. Not bad for a jellyfish! Somebody had spread the word that I was no longer a pest. The council was drawn from both the pupils and the staff, and it was supposed to organize our life at Foxhole.

Trudi was upset. At first I thought it was because I'd joined the council, which she regarded as "bourgeois and irrelevant," but it wasn't that. She must have seen my first meetings with Esther in the courtyard when, all at once, we chatted without actually arguing. She must have known that I wouldn't mention Esther's name unless I was made to. Her desk next to mine in Bridget's classroom now jerked away in the opposite direction, producing a gap between us. She made a great thing of her friendship with Martin, and with him she spoke about politics in a loud voice, telling him how the council was contrary to the interests of the working class. She also said something about lovesick council members who would be liquidated in the first days of the world revolution, but I paid no attention to that.

In the second week of February, Trudi launched a revolution against the council, which didn't surprise me. Posters appeared on the walls and slogans were chalked across the blackboards. Martin was helping her, obviously. It was quite funny to start with, but it began to go wrong when Trudi let down a banner from the dining room balcony, saying:

CRUSH THE SCHOOL COUNCIL

AND EVERY BESOTTED MEMBER THEREOF

Well, we laughed quite a lot, but then Trudi made a speech from the balcony, and that was different. She was crying, for a start. She described the council as a reactionary body composed of "the blind, the feeble and the emotionally immature." We jeered, but she just spoke louder. At last everyone was howling, and Trudi ran from the balcony waving her fists in the air.

Now Royden Clancy bent toward me. As usual, he was desperately polite. "What did she say? Was it friendly?"

"She doesn't like the council. She'd rather have a revolution."

"A revolution? In these halls?" Royden's head rolled in a circle.

"It's just Trudi going on," said Bella, who these days sat near Royden when she could.

I thought no more about the revolution until the next morning, when Martin brought a tank into the courtyard. It was a tottering affair mounted on baby-carriage wheels (saved, no doubt, from the catapult) and on the front was a poster saying CRUSH THE COUNCIL! DANIEL IS A BOURGEOIS VOLUPTUARY in scarlet letters. It rolled on to the pavement outside the assembly hall, where it came to a halt. A piece of metal fell off the back.

"A pity it keeps wobbling," Bella said.

The axles were bending under the weight, the wheels turning upwards. From the turret, where a slit had been cut, a piece of gas pipe was swinging left and right, left and right, like a gun.

"We shall fire upon counterrevolutionaries," said Martin inside the tank. "Daniel is expelled from Foxhole for moral depravity."

An acorn, catapulted from an upper window, came in a long curve and broke against the turret. Some moron was enjoying the revolution, apparently.

"Fascist hyena," said Martin.

Royden was at my elbow again. "Say, what is this thing?"

"A tank, I think."

"Would that be a *real* weapon? Boy, at this school you can do *anything.*"

Now I could see Trudi on the roof by the assembly hall. She wore her purple dress. She was making a speech, which I couldn't hear, and waving a tube of cardboard in the air. No doubt it contained a manifesto saying what a lemon I was. Oh, Trudi, I thought, what a lot of fuss to make about love!

A second acorn, and a third, came lobbing down from a high window, hitting the tank. The counterrevolutionary was making the most of it and I could hear Martin swearing inside the tank. Trudi came to the edge of the roof and called on the tank to maintain the revolution. Her face was white and her eyes red. I watched as the turret turned slowly toward the window, the gun lifting and steadying on the target.

"Holy cow!" said Royden.

"Shoot!" said Trudi. "Show no mercy!"

"The tank's coming to pieces," Bella said.

I'm not sure what happened next, but I think Martin tried to blow a mud pellet up the pipe. There was a sudden jolt, the body of the tank fell onto the concrete with a crash, and the weapon zigzagged up to the sky. A pellet rose two feet in the air and fell back again, breaking against the turret. A moment later the whole thing came apart and Martin rolled out.

"I could see it wasn't any good," Bella said, without interest.

There was a cry from Trudi and I saw her going away over the roof, holding the manifesto, if that's what it was, high in the air. The cry was awful, and it echoed in my head. The revolution was my fault, of course. I ran out of the courtyard and into the library, where it was quiet, and where I wouldn't hear it if Trudi cried again.

I walked around the library in a daze. In a space between the shelves, I came upon Esther. She kept her eyes on a book, but she knew I was there. I saw her back stiffen and wobble a bit when I didn't go away.

"Trudi's upset," I said. "She was on the roof, waving a paper."

She gave me a quick glance. "I know," she said.

"It was a manifesto or something."

"Actually, it wasn't."

Just like that. Esther turned a page, then another. She knew why Trudi had launched the revolution and what the tube of cardboard contained. Women always know everything.

"It was a bomb," she said.

"A what?"

"Trudi has made a bomb. She told me you couldn't have a revolution without a bomb." Esther tossed her head; I should've known, of course. "Trudi had kept some fireworks from the autumn. She took out the bangs and put them together in a tube. The fuse was to be a sparkler. She was going to use the bomb if the revolution failed."

My head was floating around like a balloon. "We'd better tell Curry," I said.

"I already have. He told me that Trudi was in need of friendship. He told me that she'd been disappointed in love. He went out to look for her."

I was a worm. It was obvious. "I think she's gone away, probably into the woods," I said.

Esther pretended to read the book. "She was going to blow you up with the bomb," she said, and she was nearly laughing. Probably she saw me going up for half a mile.

"It's not funny."

"No . . . well, not very."

She kept her eyes away from mine. She stroked her hair. She rolled her head on her shoulders, letting the hair wash around like a wave.

"You will have to go and look for her," she said. Oh, so superior!

"I may get blown up."

"You will have to go, anyway. I can't, of course, as I would make things worse."

She turned toward me, holding her hair back. Esther, the girl who caused a revolution! She wanted to see the flash of the bomb, to feel the rush of wind against her cheek. She wanted her hair to stream out behind her. *B-a-n-g!*

"I suppose I'll have to go," I said. "I'll have to go and find Trudi."

(Let me say, once and for all, that I'm not a hero, and certainly I didn't want to be blown up by the bomb, but I felt sorry about Trudi, particularly that she'd cried, and I wanted her brought back to Foxhole.)

"The trouble is," I went on, "I don't know where to look for her."

Esther put on her mysterious smile. That was easy. She knew where Trudi was. She had special powers. "You'll find her in North Wood," she said.

"How d'you know?"

"Sometimes she talks to me. She has a secret place in the wood. But I don't know where it is."

"In the wood. . . ."

I edged away backward, while Esther closed her eyes, seeing visions, seeing Trudi among the wet trees.

"I'm going now," I said. "I'm going to look for Trudi and the bomb."

She opened her eyes a fraction wider. She might have been frightened. But then she tossed her head casually. She wouldn't mind too much if they brought me back *in pieces.*

I went down to the Old Postern, from where I followed a path into North Wood. The wood was huge, covering the top of a hill, and on the far side it fell toward the river.

Rain was falling now. Overhead the clouds were low and racing in the wind. The trees were shaking, the branches making a soft noise. The school had sent out other searchers, and at one moment I heard voices calling "Trudi! Trudi!" (Can you believe it? They thought she would answer!) Then they were gone, and their voices were covered by the dripping of the trees and the hiss of the river as it washed over stones at the bottom of the hill.

I was sure she was in the wood, as Esther had said. Only by waiting, silently, would I see her. I found a place where the branches grew close together, like an umbrella, and there I crouched while the rain fell all around and the shadows grew thicker.

I waited for an hour. More, I think. Meanwhile I heard the scamper of rabbits and once, in the distance, the barking of a dog. The rain died out. When the light faded, a mist came, touching my cheeks and hands, filling the gaps in the forest and spreading over the river.

Then I jumped up. I could hear her crying. I listened to a sob, wondering if it could be the rain. After a time I was sure it was Trudi's voice and that she was on the high ground behind me. All along she'd been quite close. For some reason I wanted to cry as well. I started toward her, moving as quietly as I could, but I heard her scramble up and run away through the bushes. Farther on, in a gap between the trees, I caught sight of her; I saw a smudge of purple darting this way and that, and I saw the whiteness of her face as she glanced, terrified, over her shoulder.

"Trudi," I called. "It's only Daniel."

I can't say how she got through the trees while I crashed into branches and became tied up in thorns. She was carried away on wings and in a minute I'd lost her. I plunged on under the dripping trees, seeing no one.

87

Then I stopped, out of breath, somewhere on the path leading down to the Old Postern. There was movement nearby.

"Daniel?" she said. "Is it Daniel?"

I turned. She was a little darker than the trees. "Just me," I said.

Had she gone? No, I could still see her.

"It's cold in the wood," I said. "You'd better come back."

"Why? You don't like me anymore. Not *now*."

I couldn't answer that. You see, I never *had* liked Trudi very much. I'd only put up with her because she was pathetic.

She said something else, about my lack of intellectual development, but the river-sound blotted most of it out, and then she stood there crying. At least, I think she was crying, but it might have been the wind in the leaves. I wondered what I should do. If I made a dash toward her, she would run away faster than I could manage. I wasn't much of a runner, to be frank. Talk, I supposed. Say something, anything.

"We all enjoyed the revolution," I said. "We'll have another later on."

"It's not over," Trudi said, and she passed something from one hand to the other. Something about the size and shape of a rolling pin. *The bomb.* She was still carrying the bomb!

"The tank fell apart. They've taken down the posters."

I was edging my way up the hill toward Trudi, slowly, hoping she wouldn't see me. I meant to get near enough for a flying tackle before she could light the bomb. I'd actually made a couple of yards before she spotted what I was doing, and then she ran back a long way, farther than before.

Her voice was in the distance now. "Go away, Daniel! Go back to that girl you're so stuck on."

I was silly enough to ask, "Which girl?"

"The one with dark eyes."

"Oh," I said.

"THE ONE YOU'RE IN LOVE WITH!"

Now Trudi was telling the whole of North Wood about Esther and me, her voice echoing in the trees. I was embarrassed and ready to run away. I walked in a circle, kicking the leaves. I'd never said such a thing, even to myself. Then I remembered what I was doing and I looked again at the patch of purple way up the path. I was really sorry for Trudi, who had frizzy hair and bow legs, and I wanted her to come in out of the mist.

"Let's go home," I said.

No answer.

Not a word!

I thought I was still looking at Trudi, who was standing there, watching me, but when I climbed the path I found it empty. I cried for a minute or two, there in the mist. Then I went down to the Old Postern, from where I rang up Foxhole and told them that Trudi was in North Wood.

They didn't find Trudi that night, though search parties went into the wood on every path. She was lost in the mist, together with the bomb. (We found out later that she had crossed the river at Staverton and walked most of the way to Buckfastleigh.) The following day there were strong winds, with cloud shadows chasing over the courtyard.

And early that morning, Trudi came back, walking

across the playing fields toward Foxhole. She came not in a straight line but swinging left and right, kicking things in the grass and speaking to someone who wasn't there. In one hand she carried the bomb. With Curry and Bridget, I went down from the school and waited by the gate. Esther was at the top of the steps behind us, partly hidden by the branches. When she saw us, Trudi sat down in the wet grass, the bomb at her side.

"Why not come in, Trudi dear?" Curry asked.

She said nothing that I heard.

"You need a hot bath," Bridget said. "Daniel is here. All your friends want you to come in."

"Daniel's a vile deviationist," Trudi said, and cried.

"We will use no force," Curry promised her, "but I will be grateful if you will listen to argument."

Of course, to *argument.* This was Dartington, after all.

I could see someone on the far side of the playing field, where a lane ran between high banks toward the Old Postern. Someone, bending over, had skirted the field to cut off Trudi's retreat. Someone who didn't care much about argument. I watched him leap the bank and run toward Trudi with his arms stretched wide, ready to snatch her from the grass. Ossi Nin, at full pelt.

"Oh dear," said Bridget.

No one could say that Trudi wasn't smart. A moment before Ossi reached her, she jumped to one side, taking the bomb with her, while Ossi ran past the place where she'd been and continued for six huge strides, until he fell flat on his face and skidded toward us. Trudi had meanwhile darted into the small pavilion on our right.

"Nearly I have her," said Ossi. "Now she has gone away with the bomb."

"It might have been better if you'd waited," Curry said.

We stared at the small, square, wooden pavilion where Trudi had gone with the bomb. Esther came down the steps, looking rather pale. She glanced at me once. If you can believe it, she was pleased to find me *still alive.*

"I will speak to Trudi," Curry said. "Finally she must be amenable to reason."

"By now the bomb is made harmless by the rain," said Ossi. He'd gone into one of his sulks when he failed to catch Trudi.

Curry walked toward the pavilion. The sun came out, putting a dazzle in the wet grass and giving me the impression that nothing would happen. In fact, I went on thinking that nothing would happen even when something did.

Trudi burst out of the pavilion with the smoking bomb held above her head. We all gasped and jumped up and down on the spot. After a moment, Curry ran after her. He looked very funny running on short legs behind Trudi. They followed a swerving course until, somewhere in the middle of the field, there was an orange flash and both figures disappeared in a cloud of black smoke that billowed outward from a fiery center. The sound of the explosion (*phut,* actually) reached us at the gate half a second later.

"So it went off," Ossi said, still lying in the grass at the end of a long skid mark, "but it was much reduced by the rain."

"I will help them in," said Bridget.

9

THE WIND AND THE RAIN GAVE OUT AT THE end of March. You could see new leaves on the trees, and fresh grass along the banks of the Dart. There was nothing left of the winter but fallen branches and, now that I think of it, a black stain in the middle of the sports field where Trudi's bomb had gone off, but that got smaller as the weeks passed, until it disappeared altogether.

At this time I began to look for Esther in the courtyard after my music lesson. Usually she was there, throwing a ball. Then she would come with me, no matter which way I was going. I never asked her, and she'd have said No if I had. We would leave Foxhole and take one of the paths through the woods not saying much. I hadn't touched her since the night of the snow and usually we walked a yard apart.

When the woods dried out, we went farther off, crossing the fields to North Wood, where the chestnuts were already covered in leaves and the beeches were beginning to go green. The tracks, slushy all winter, had grown hard, and even the dangerous path along the edge of the river was safe enough if you went carefully. Here at first the river ran over stones, but farther down, where the trees grew thickly, the banks were steeper and the current ran hardly at all.

At last, at a place called Still Pool, where moss-covered rocks surrounded an inlet, the flow had stopped altogether and the water was black and still. Even the trees around the pool were usually quiet.

Esther liked to stop at Still Pool and look into the water. "No one's ever reached the bottom," she said one afternoon. "Did you know that?"

I dropped a stone into the water and it vanished after a second.

"I think about it at night," Esther said. "I think about what it would be like to sink lower and lower in the water, never reaching the bottom."

Her eyes fell back to the water. I could see the side of her face and how her nose was dead straight and the cheeks smooth and a little hollow. I knew she was afraid, because her lips were trembling, but it wasn't just the river that frightened her. She'd gone a long way off, forgetting that I was beside her, and I felt lonely, deserted, as I had in autumn when she didn't come back to Dartington.

I picked up a stone and hurled it across the river.

"What's the matter?" Esther asked, alarmed. She turned to me, her eyes large and dark and startled. Now she was more frightened still and I didn't know why. "I'll go walking with someone else if you're going to be angry."

93

"I don't want you to," I said. The idea bothered me. With my mind's eye I saw her in the distance, walking with someone else, someone I didn't like very much, and they were close together.

"Martin, for instance," Esther said. (God, she knew how to get me going!)

I sat beside her. I was frightened myself, now. I got the crazy idea that if I closed my eyes and held them shut Esther would have gone when I opened them. There'd be nothing beside me but emptiness. And in fact I *did* shut my eyes for a second, and opened them again, and of course Esther was still there, looking just as she had a moment before.

We said nothing for a time. Whatever it was that frightened Esther, the great black *thing,* had now wrapped itself around us both like a blanket. I was trembling as much as she was. I began to think of the place she came from, which she'd never talk about, and I started asking questions I hadn't asked before. It was silly, but I did it anyway.

"Tell me about the place you come from," I said.

She shook her head, her mouth tight shut.

(I knew where she came from, of course. Ages ago Bridget had told me that Esther came from Vienna and that her parents were Austrian intellectuals, but I'd never mentioned it before.)

"It's Vienna, isn't it?"

"If you know, why do you ask me?" Her voice was sad, not angry.

"What's it like in Vienna?"

"I don't want to talk about it."

"Why ever not?" I was getting into a state, my ears humming. I wanted to know everything about Esther.

94

"Stop shouting."

"I'm not shouting."

She said, her voice all over the place, "Vienna's very clean and tidy. The houses are painted bright colors. Last month it was occupied by Hitler."

She was breathing heavily and I think sobbing a bit. I'd gone too far. Daniel, the great comforter.

"I'm sorry," I said.

"My father went back to Vienna two weeks ago," she went on. "He's an anti-Fascist, you see. Mother came here to tell me."

"Why'd he do that?"

"He has to fight Hitler. Mother said he was very brave. She intends to follow him."

"I expect they'll come back soon."

"Maybe. . . ."

"Don't you think so?"

She looked into Still Pool and her eyes reflected the dark water. "I don't know what will happen."

She'd gone away from me again, back to the dangerous place she came from. I said, "I don't see my parents much, either. Mother spends most of her time in France and my father has a flat in New York."

Her eyes rose to my face and she looked at me for a long time. "Then you'll know how I feel," she said.

Her eyes were kind. We weren't fighting any more. My ears stopped humming and I could hear the sound of the river and a bird singing in the wood. Esther was still buzzing a bit, which was some sort of warning, but soon that stopped as well and I listened to her breath as it rustled over her lips. I wanted to take hold of her, but she would not have liked that. Instead, I let my shoulder fall an inch toward hers (she was quite close) and I turned my head in her direction. We didn't say anything, and I couldn't have put into words what I felt, anyway.

Both of us had come to a stop. I let my shoulder fall another inch nearer and she did the same. A moment later our shoulders were just touching, as if they'd drifted together in a crowd. We stayed like that for a long time. Neither of us was frightened anymore. The minutes crept past like giants on tiptoe until I lost count of time.

Later we went to a favorite place.

Beech Tree Bridge, as we called it, was a still-living tree that had fallen across the stream some winters ago. It was possible to walk along the trunk toward the middle of the river until you reached the upper branches, which grew both into the water and toward the sky. Esther ran down the length of the tree. I followed behind her, slowly, holding on where I could. I was just the sort of person to fall in. The new leaves were showing now, even though they were still half folded and not very green. At the end, where the water made a slight sound as it ran through the branches below, we sat on the old smooth trunk and reached toward the surface with our hands.

We didn't speak much. The lapping of the river was like another voice, one that did the talking for us. Esther dangled her leg over the side of the tree, searching for the water with her toe. Her leg was rather thin, but there was down over the thigh and the light from the water made it shine. I would not have known that time was passing but for the sight of a leaf that was moving with the current—that, and the sound of Esther's breath, which sometimes I couldn't separate from the river's sound.

I was happy on the beech tree with Esther, but it didn't last long.

Minutes later I heard voices on the path and looked down the Dart toward Still Pool. And there, far off, I saw a smear of red behind the leaves, and the flash of a white cap, as a noisy couple came up the path. They didn't lower their voices as we had done. They crashed over things, laughing. Birds flew up from the rushes and a vole shot like an arrow to the opposite bank.

Bella in scarlet shorts, Royden in his cap. We hid behind the thin cover of the leaves. They stopped at Still Pool and we heard their voices across the water.

"They say it's haunted," Bella said, and she made a shivering noise.

"Aw—hell—do they?" said Royden.

Esther gave a furious hiss. "She's not really frightened," she said.

"They'll go away in a minute."

But they stayed at the edge of the pool, seating themselves where, only a short time earlier, we had sat together and our shoulders had touched. They were rubbing us out even before we'd gone away.

"I'm frightened," Bella said contentedly.

"There, there!"

"I'm shaking all over."

I altered my position, bringing them behind an opening in the leaves. Bella was lying full length on the ground, her scarlet shorts undone at the top, and Royden was bending over her.

"Why must they do it there?" Esther asked.

"It doesn't matter," I said. But I knew that it did.

"I suppose they're *in love*," Esther said disgustedly.

97

(I should explain that, at Dartington, being "in love" meant no more than a decision to go around together and sometimes to kiss. Lovers swapped over quite often. Bella and Royden seemed to be "in love" at the moment, but that obviously included some messing about as well.)

"It looks like it," I said.

In fact, Bella looked like something spilled on the ground, something that had splashed in all directions. Esther turned away, frowning. She put her shoulders up round her ears and hugged her arms together. She rocked from side to side and gave a sort of moan. Something had gone terribly wrong. I wanted to ask her what it was, but I was too scared. The great black *thing* had come back again.

I turned and looked up the Dart toward Staverton. There the light was flashing as the current broke over the stones. I was sick of Royden and Bella and the noise they made. And in fact they must have gone soon afterward, climbing up through the woods, for though I listened I couldn't hear them.

Esther shook her head. She took a deep breath and blew it out again. She said, her voice breaking up, "They reminded me of something. . . ."

"What?"

"Something at home, when I was a child."

I waited for her to go on.

"There were young people from Germany walking all over Austria. Young people in shorts. They called themselves the Hitler Youth and they did things like that."

"I see," I said.

"They made great fires. They sang loud songs. I was frightened of them."

"Well, they won't come *here*," I said, without really believing it. "England's different."

Her eyes flared. "Soon they'll be everywhere," she said.

I tried not to think about it, but in a minute I was caught up in Esther's dream. I saw troops of young people, all in shorts, all singing, all looking like Royden and Bella. I saw them coming along the river path and around the corner toward the beech tree. Ranks and ranks of them. Then, when I added a band and a lot of banners, I got even more worked up than Esther. I broke twigs off the tree and dropped them into the water, where they drifted away toward the dark part of the river downstream.

"About Martin . . . ," I began. The afternoon was spoiled anyway, so I might as well mess it up thoroughly.

"What about him?"

"I don't like him much, though he's supposed to be my friend. Please don't go walking with him."

She looked into my face, like a flashlight beam. "I didn't mean that I *would* go with Martin, only that I *could* if I wanted. Actually, I *don't* want to," Esther said.

I felt a little better, but not much.

"There's so little time," she said, her voice softer than before. "So little time. Soon we'll both have to leave Dartington and it's unlikely we'll see each other again, *ever*."

"I suppose that's true."

"Sit beside me, Danny, please," Esther said.

I sat beside her, looking down the river to where the stream vanished under the trees, in a swirl of darkness.

❧ 10 ❧

OF THAT SUMMER I REMEMBER BEST HOW THE
sun shone in the fields around Foxhole and caught the
drift of thistledown across the orchards. In the first week
of the term the swimming pool by the woods was filled,
bringing the dragonflies up from the Bidwell, and we
plunged in, no matter that it was cold. Soon, though, it
grew warmer, and the trees filled out so that the pool was
hidden—which was just as well, because we bathed with
nothing on, and Dartington already had a bad name in the
district, where they said we were shameless.

That summer I had a room on the upper floor looking
into the courtyard. The window was open at night and I
could hear footsteps on the paved walkway below. So
much at Dartington went on after dark! For instance, I
knew that Royden was crossing the courtyard to Bella's

room on the ground floor. The trouble he took to hide his visits made them more obvious. I would hear him open his window, and then I'd see the white cap floating about in the dark below. He crossed the grass with huge silent steps, his finger to his lips, saying, "Hush!" In getting through Bella's window he managed, nearly always, to get stuck halfway, his legs waving about, but after a bit he would zoom through when Bella gave an enormous tug on the inside.

The afternoons were warm, and often Professor Bolski continued my lesson until past five o'clock, forgetting the time, but always, in the end, he gathered our manuscripts together with a flutter of apology. Then, still carrying the sounds in my head, I went out into the garden and down to the lawns and the pool, where Esther always waited, usually alone, carrying our towels. We sat on the grass bank above the pool, not speaking. Here by the wood there were new, different sounds—the chatter of birds, the small noises the trees made, the splash of water falling into the pool.

We undressed on the bank, letting our clothes fall any-where on the grass. I didn't look at her, but I knew that her skin had a sheen upon it and that the line of her black hair cut sharply across her naked shoulders. I didn't touch her. I didn't *breathe* upon her, for that matter, because I was frightened she might vanish, as she had the summer before, and never come back. She was just a shadow thrown by the sun and could disappear as quickly.

Her body was still slim, like a boy's, with the bones barely covered, with hardly a shadow between her breasts. She went into the pool by the steps, the water breaking and rippling and showing a wobbly reflection of her face as she peered into the depths. She swam away from the side, with

101

small, hurried strokes, the sun flashing in the water. Usually she called me to join her and I went tumbling in, with a great upheaval of the pool, and she fled to the side, where she dashed the water from her eyes, and smiled, and hid her face from the splashes.

We never stayed long in the pool but scrambled out to lie on the bank in the orange light, not touching or speaking, just letting the warm air blow over us until we were dry, and then, quite casually, rising to dress again.

I remember a moment from early that summer. I remember it better than anything else about Esther. It came one evening when we rose from the grass, when the sun was still warm and the wind was hardly moving at all. We hadn't picked up our clothes. Suddenly she was looking at me, her eyes wide. And in the same way my eyes were caught by hers. For a time her pale figure blurred and she became strange. Now she was somebody else, older, wiser than me. Somebody who'd moved on and was now so beautiful it made me dizzy. I saw the darkness of her eyes and the slight lifting of her breast.

"Hello," I said, though she'd been there all the time.

"Hello," Esther replied.

After a while she turned her head away, violently, and searched for the little bits of clothing that lay on the bank. There was nothing for us to say. We walked away from the pool in silence, our shadows long on the grass, the late sun lying across the yellow buildings of Dartington.

About this time I showed Professor Bolski my first writing for the piano. He had asked me for a set of variations on a theme we had composed together, and I had worked on it in the holiday. He took the pages from me and looked at them with his head on one side, nervously. He read the piece through and then sat tapping the sheets with his spectacles.

"It's rotten, isn't it?" I said.

"No."

"Dreadful, if you ask me."

He didn't reply but placed the music on the stand. He struck the first chords lightly, as if the manuscript puzzled him, but he put some guts into the principal subject. After that he went sailing on, making something of those passages that were flat or just awful, but to me the piece sounded patchy and dull.

"Let's throw it out," I said.

"Daniel, you must have patience. You have been working for only a year. There is much here of originality. The second variation has great melodic charm."

"Schultz would have done it better."

"Daniel—dear Daniel—Schultz wouldn't have written like this at all. In his hands this theme would have been entirely of the Continent, with many tensions and strange harmonies. You are English, and therefore you have given it an open melody which touches me deeply."

He returned to the piano and played the second variation again. He was speaking as he played. "The question may be impertinent, but tell me what you were thinking when you wrote this passage."

"Me? Thinking? Nothing, really."

"I find that strange. Indeed, I dare to disbelieve you. Such delightedness must spring from experience. Or, shall I say, from some person?"

"Oh, well. . . ."

"Enough, enough! I have worked with composers too long to ask them the source of their inspiration when they don't wish to reveal it." All at once he stopped playing and folded his hands. "But, Daniel, you must not be afraid of darker subjects. Music requires shadow as well as light. Not all of it springs from happiness—"

"I've never thought that."

"—or from a girl's promise of great beauty."

I went to the window and stared at the garden outside.

"Now I have angered you. Forgive me, Daniel! Realize that I come from Europe, where the shadows are already great and war cannot be long delayed. I dare say you will have a share in Europe's misfortune before long."

"I expect so."

"The little girl is already involved in Austria's distress."

I caught my breath. Tears were pricking my eyes.

"These things will make a difference to your music. It will be deepened in quality if you regard them fearlessly."

I said, "Shall we get on?"

"Very well. We get on." Bolski got back to business by sitting up straight and twitching his shoulders. "We get on, no matter that the world grows more ugly and already Europe is littered with unmarked graves. I will play these variations at the next school concert, but first you must change the order of the music to give a better development."

He pressed the pages against the music rest and attacked them with a pencil, calling me sharply to his elbow.

I can't remember when the rumors began but it must have been toward the end of that term. We were startled and a little shocked. (It was odd for anyone at Dartington to be shocked.) Such a thing had never happened before, we said very seriously.

Bella was removed to the sick room, and someone passing below the windows told us that she was crying. We asked Bridget if we could visit Bella and she said No, not at present. Bella would come back very soon, Bridget said. Meanwhile, Royden walked round the corridors with his head drooping. He looked like a handful of sodden washing. "God, they'll hang me," was all that he said.

It may have been Royden's stupid affair that gave Curry the idea of talking to me. He sent for me one day late in the term. I'd done nothing wrong that I could remember and I couldn't think why he wanted me now. He greeted me with a lot of smiles and showed me to a chair.

He sat beside me, took out his pipe and filled it. "What age are you now, Daniel?" he asked.

"Fifteen."

"And you are enjoying Dartington?"

"Oh—yes."

He made a great show of lighting the pipe. He was a small, round man and the smoke nearly blotted him out. Then he started off about sex, speaking in a quiet voice, every now and again returning to the pipe and making a sucking noise. He told me nothing we hadn't covered with the biology instructor, David Lack. He was talking more to himself than to me and I found him a little boring. So instead of listening I studied the large reproduction of the *Sunflowers*, which hung over the fireplace.

"You have heard me, Daniel?"

"We did all this with Lack."

"But the subject is of interest to you?"

"I found it interesting when Lack described it. But when Bella got pregnant I thought it just . . . silly."

He gave a lot of attention to the pipe, looking at it from different angles. "At Dartington, we don't wish to intrude in the private affairs of young people," he went rolling on. "We make no attempt to limit friendships, but you may

105

agree it does no harm to discuss them rationally. Esther, of course, is nearly a year younger than you, and it would be more usual for her to form a friendship with someone from her own group."

He paused, but it didn't seem to be a question.

"Well?" I asked.

"I was hoping you would tell me about your relationship with her."

"There's nothing to say."

"Really? You are with her a great deal."

Royden had got him going, of course. With my thumb about eighteen inches from my eye, I traced the edge of the *Sunflowers*, taking a long time.

"You are fond of Esther?"

"She's all right."

"And you find her beautiful?"

"Not bad."

"It's always best to speak frankly, Daniel. Esther is a beautiful child in anyone's opinion. As you know, her father is an eminent Austrian who has recently gone home to denounce the Anschluss."

"The what?"

"Hitler's assumption of power in his country."

"Oh."

"Her mother has now followed him, which leaves Esther in my care. Why is it, Daniel, that you are not ready to talk about Esther?"

I didn't know. I knew only that his questions annoyed me. "Can I go now?" I asked.

"I would prefer you to stay. I accept that Esther has a meaning for you that other girls have not. I would like you to tell me what that is."

"I'm not doing her any harm."

"I didn't say you were, but the other night you were with her at the pool for nearly an hour. I have to be certain that she's all right."

"I haven't messed about with her, if that's what you mean."

"You have not?"

I said No very loudly, and his head jumped away from me. "Why can't you believe me? Esther's not like Bella."

My ears were singing. I saw no reason to answer his questions even if I could. After the night in the snow, I hadn't wanted to touch Esther particularly, though at Beech Tree Bridge I had liked the sight of her naked leg when the sun caught the hollow in the thigh; I had watched it as she dipped her toe toward the water, her skirt slipping up, with the sounds of the river all around. But I *hadn't* touched her, and that made it no business of Curry's.

I said, "I haven't done anything wrong. *God!*"

"You will learn," Curry continued, smooth as smooth, "that I have never condemned any sexual interest that a young person may admit to. But I believe in total candor."

He waited for me to speak, to describe my feelings for Esther, but even to speak her name would have been more than I could do.

"Very well. I shall have to consider taking Esther away from Foxhole and keeping her with me at High Cross—"

"No!"

"You leave me no alternative."

"Don't take her away!"

"Daniel, she may in any case leave before the end of the term to join her parents in Vienna. I have a letter—"

"But she'll come back in the autumn, won't she? They won't keep her in Vienna?"

107

"I imagine she will return, but the matter is not in my hands. It will help me if you will speak freely."

I hadn't expected Professor Bolski to come barging in, but at that moment he did. All of a sudden, there he was in the middle of the carpet! He was rocking on his feet.

"What is this about the little girl?" Bolski asked, his accent heavier than usual. "What is it you are planning?"

Curry held his pipe a mile from his mouth, but it was the only sign of surprise he gave.

"They tell me in the common room that you will take the little girl away from Daniel."

"If you wish to discuss it," Curry said, "I suggest a separate interview."

"I discuss it now. This is not possible."

"Professor, you seem to have forgotten that I have a right to make decisions at Dartington."

But Bolski had run out of steam, in any case, and he made awkward movements with his feet. "I am sorry. I am sorry that I intrude. But the matter is of concern to me."

"You'd better take a chair," Curry said.

Instead, Bolski went all around the carpet, coming back to where he started. He said, "The boy has a talent and you will destroy it."

"I think that unlikely. It is our aim at Dartington to exploit talent."

"It cannot be exploited in this way."

Curry was silent, his head bent over his hands, his eyes fixed on Bolski.

"His gift will diminish if the girl is taken away. She is necessary. Or perhaps it dies altogether. I do not know."

"I cannot think only of Daniel's talent, Professor."

"He will not hurt her. How could he? He would destroy

his gift in the same moment. In this, I understand Daniel better than you."

"She's only fourteen. We've already had one incident which could damage the school severely."

"That was not the same."

Curry's eyes grew wider. "You will have to convince me of the difference, Professor."

"Daniel has written some passages of real beauty. He knows well enough where they come from. They are written in praise, in celebration, and no composer will destroy the source of his music. That is what makes Daniel different from the other boy. Forgive me, but you have judged him wrongly."

Curry pulled at his pipe, thinking about Esther and me, disappearing in a cloud of smoke, while inside my head I was saying, *Let her stay, let her stay!* and Bolski was tying his hands in a knot.

Esther stayed at Foxhole. I wasn't a depraved monster, after all. But I still had the impression that something would go wrong. I would blink my eyes, and Esther would be gone.

Bella came back some days later. There wasn't a clap of thunder or anything like that—just Bella in the courtyard, wearing the same blue skirt with a hole in it we'd seen before. She went about the school without seeing us, her eyes like mud. When she passed Royden in the corridor and their shoulders bumped together, she paid him no attention and just continued on her way.

They didn't hang Royden, though he was in Curry's study for an hour. When he came out, his knees had gone and his mouth was hanging open. "I can stay," he told us outside, "as long as I don't do *that* again. But *did I get hell!*"

❧11❧

ONE SNEEZE AND SHE WOULD BE GONE. I COULD
only see it that way. I had this feeling strongly when, one
weekend near the end of the term, we went with David
Lack to watch the sea birds on the estuary of the Dart. This
was at Dittisham, where the river widened out between
wooded banks before reaching the sea at Dartmouth. The
tide was down and the sun was brilliant in the mud as we
walked beside the estuary.

I don't remember what birds we saw, but the sky was full
of them, soaring and gliding and coming down far out on
the water.

Esther had walked away from me, going a long way down
the shore until she was no more than a pencil stroke where
the river bent toward Dartmouth. I told myself she'd
turn the corner and disappear altogether. I sat in the grass,

watching her, as the others fooled around at the edge of the mud. Martin, of course, fell in, and I heard the sloshing noise as they pulled him out, but I didn't look; I was watching Esther as she stood on the point a hundred yards away. Then she turned and came back toward me, slowly.

She wandered up to me, as if nothing had happened. She gave a nod that was so small I nearly missed it: she was telling me that I was right, that she was going, vanishing, almost at once.

"Don't say it," I said.

She gave a dark smile. And after that I got the stupid idea that if I said nothing, thought nothing, the whole thing would go away. So I made my mind a blank, held my breath for as long as I could, and watched the tide running out.

"Martin's in an awful mess," she said.

(Say nothing, do nothing!)

"I think he did it on purpose."

The falling tide had made ridges in the mud. A wind over the estuary was rippling the distant water, where the gulls were bobbing.

"I leave tomorrow," Esther said.

"I know. I guessed."

"I shall be in Austria for some months."

I watched a gull curving down to join the other gulls, beating its wings as it settled on the water.

"I don't want you to go," I said.

Something in my voice (I was probably blubbing) made Esther lift her head. Her eyes were hollow and there were tears along the bottom edge. Quickly she wiped her eyes with the back of her hand.

"My parents want it. I shall have to go," she said.

"You'll be back in the autumn, of course."

111

"I don't know. They haven't said."

I looked at my feet. As far as I was concerned, she'd already gone, leaving me beside the muddy river.

I said, "They never say. They don't tell you anything."

I could hear Esther moving about close by and, some yards away, the noise Martin was making as they rubbed the mud off. "I shall miss you," I said.

She left me then, saying nothing, her shadow falling away and the sun striking through the space where she had been.

When we returned from the holiday in September, Esther wasn't there. I walked on my own, often going further than I meant. After my music lesson there were hours of daylight left, and I would walk and walk until, somewhere, I was blocked by the river. Usually I stared into the water, which was shiny black with nothing breaking the surface but the trout rings. Sometimes I sat on Beech Tree Bridge, finding the same place in the branches every time, listening to the bells of Staverton church as they struck one quarter after another. I looked through the yellowing leaves to Still Pool, now shadowy, with no one there, until the darkness wiped it all out and a cold air came lapping up from the water.

Soon the river was fuller, bringing down leaves and tugging at the bank. It had rained on the moors, so now the streams were bursting and the Dart had risen until it pulled at the willows. Then it rained every day. Usually the rain caught me a long way from Foxhole, and I would walk on, in a little hollow in the storm, with the rain stinging my eyes. I returned wet through so many times my housemother told me I was mad and likely to get pneumonia.

112

What else can I remember from that autumn term? Trudi, for a start. She was sad, her eyes murky. Since her revolution months ago she'd kept mostly to herself. We knew that her father had disappeared in Germany. That was nothing out of the ordinary, we said, just the sort of thing that happened in Europe, where things always got worse, not better.

I was surprised one day when Trudi came bouncing into the courtyard, her face bright as a button. "Tell me about your music, Daniel. It is good, yes? It makes you happy?" But the brightness flickered out almost at once. "Go to America if you can," she said. "Your father, I know, is already there. In Europe there is nothing for you."

Then Trudi took hold of my coat with one hand, and when I backed away she grabbed me with the other, bringing herself close to me and breathing at me. Her watery eyes turned up to my face.

"I know you don't like me very much. It doesn't matter. Save yourself if you can."

Her wet lips touched my cheek. It was more of a splash than a kiss. Then she swung away from me, crying, and bolted back indoors.

Europe. I tried not to think of it but it kept coming back. There was a mist hanging over it where lost people wandered about. I was frightened, I think, particularly at night when the window was dark and the whole place silent.

"No one comes back," Martin said, on the last night of term. "They just disappear."

I tried to hit him but he dodged away, laughing. I went out into the dark, where it was cold and the sky was high and spotted by stars. I walked violently away from Foxhole—going where, I wasn't sure. I went under the trees in

113

Bluebell Wood and followed the path toward the mill, down the slope, out of sight. For a time the lights showed through the trees behind me and I hurried on until the overlapping branches put out the last gleam. Then I stopped, frightened of the dark. I could feel my heart beating. I said some words, but I didn't know what they meant or who was supposed to hear them. I looked up through the branches to the nearest stars and said a whole lot more, but they got lost in the distance. I walked on, hitting trees, jumping away from shadows. Then I thought I'd go back, find Martin, and beat him till his eyes popped out, but I stayed in the bitter cold, kicking dead leaves until the rattle of my teeth drove me back up the path. One light showed through the tangle of trees. Then more. At last the windows of Foxhole were blazing in front of me and, from all over the place, I heard excited voices marking the end of term.

I stood at the edge of the wood, looking at the school. The words inside my head had turned to a single sentence, which I kept repeating: "Bring her back *Bring her back . . .*"

I went in and sat on a radiator in the lobby, listening to the footsteps in the passages beyond. They were bringing trunks down the stairs, and some jellyfish let his slide down like a toboggan. I didn't hear Bridget come in, nor did I notice her when she spoke to me. Only when she bent over me, repeating my name, did I raise my eyes, wondering what she wanted.

She spoke softly, so that no one else should hear. "I looked for you everywhere. I had to speak to you before the vacation."

"Yes. *Yes?*"

"She will return in the new year. Now I suggest you go for a bath, as you seem quite frozen."

❦12❦

HER EYES HAD CHANGED. THEY WERE LARGER,
deeper, and they moved more slowly. Now she was as tall
as I was, her breasts were round and very good, and she
walked with a swish. (Oh, how stately can you get!) She was
tidy, and I was not. And while in the summer she'd been
younger than me, now I could not be sure. She wasn't any
age. She giggled; it may have been because I was a mess.
We stood facing each other in the corridor and I shifted
my weight from one foot to the other.

"What have you been doing?" she asked me.

"Oh, this and that. Music."

"Are you pleased to see me?"

"It's all right."

(Why did I say that? I was all churned up at seeing her
again.)

Her smile was different, more resigned, the corners of her mouth just lifting, her eyes turning to the floor. She raised one hand, the fingers opening helplessly. She was telling me it was not her fault that she'd missed last term— that she couldn't help it if her bust had come out, making her better looking than anyone else. She was *apologizing,* if you can believe it!

I shook my head to stop the blood rushing about inside. "I don't suppose you'll want to walk anymore," I said.

(Trust Daniel, the boy wonder, to mess things up!)

Her eyes showed a spark of the old temper. "Why wouldn't I?"

"I mean, you'll want to do other things."

"What things?"

"See other people," I said, ready to jump off a cliff. "Martin, even."

She moved toward the door, not sharply but with the new swishing walk, and went into the courtyard. I tumbled out behind her into the wintry sunlight.

I watched her glide away from me, saw how the sun gave a bright edge to her hair. "I'm so busy with music, anyway. . . ."

She spun back to me, her hair flying. "Look, if you want to be sensible and not stupid, why not let me hear some of your music? This is just childish."

I nodded weakly. I was a crumb, of course. I led the way to a practice room, where I seated myself at the piano. She stood on one side, her arms on the lid, her head bent forward. Her eyes were dark and serious, her lips just apart. I could not believe that any of my music was as beautiful as she was and I began to go mad again.

"Play me the piece you're most proud of," Esther said.

116

I played Liszt's *Dance of Death* with a lot of thundering in the bass.

"That's not your music, Daniel. I don't know what's happened to you. Once, you were easy to get on with."

I went on playing the Liszt. "What was it like in Vienna?"

"Well, it wasn't nice, if you want to know. The Blackshirts were everywhere in the streets."

I ended the Liszt with a series of colossal chords. I might as well have broken the furniture.

Esther said, taking no notice, "My father thought an Austrian school would be unsuitable, so he sent me back here. He didn't come himself, neither did Mother. They have made a home in Vienna. Why are you so bad-tempered?"

I'd no idea, really, except that I was a messy schoolboy who'd somehow got left behind.

"I'm not bad-tempered," I said.

Her eyes, very severe, were glued to my face. I put my fingers back on the keyboard. Always, Esther could make me do what she wanted.

"That's better. Now play me something of your own."

I started a short piece, a rhapsody, but I'd only played ten bars when the life went out of it with a rush and I ran my fingers down the notes to the bottom. I put my head in my hands.

"I don't know what you're crying about," Esther said, her words quite firm and not particularly angry. "You're much too old for that sort of thing."

I felt the draft on my cheek as she went sailing out. *S-w-i-s-h!* I heard the door open, and then close softly.

* * *

She was throwing a ball in the courtyard, hitting the wall high up, clapping her hands behind her back, then catching it again. Her skirt was red with a black edge and it flowed nicely around her legs. She knew I was sitting on the steps behind her, but she didn't look at me.

I was so wrapped up in Esther, I didn't see Trudi coming across the courtyard. "Daniel," she said, "will you come with me?"

I followed her through the hall and into the forecourt. Here Martin passed us, high up on stilts, going toward the drive. He was walking around Foxhole as many times as he could before he fell off. We sat on the low wall under the clock tower while Martin went down the hill toward the gate, wobbling.

She laughed nervously. "Will you listen, Daniel, if I tell you what it's like to be a foreigner, even at Dartington?"

"If you want me to."

She blushed a little, and her lips tried a number of beginnings. She was encouraged because I hadn't put a bucket over her head. Then she told me how it felt to live in a country where you didn't quite belong, where nothing was totally familiar, where the woods and fields were not *yours* but the property of other people. "For the first time in your life you are different," Trudi said. "You are left with nothing but your memories and your pride."

There was shouting on the path behind us, where Martin was coming back into view. A crowd of young children, like a bow wave, was already in sight at the corner of the building. We saw his long shadow on the path and then, towering in height, Martin himself. *Well done, Martin!* He strode past us into the forecourt.

"This morning Esther came to my room," Trudi went on. "She complained about the rudeness of English people

118

and how little they understood the position of the refugee—"

"But Dartington's full of refugees. It's nothing new."

"Please listen! Esther thought I would understand. I *did*,
of course. I knew what it was like to feel lost in a country
and how one needed to find friends there. I *knew* . . .
though I wasn't too patient with her."

"Why not?"

"Why do you ask? It's obvious, isn't it?" Now her voice
was shrill, and I saw the tears in her eyes and the trembling
of her upper lip (which was dark and hairy, if you really
want to know). "I'd like slim legs like Esther's. I'd like hair
that didn't stick up straight. I don't really want to be *awful*,
as it happens. . . ."

For a while she was just sniffing, and from the far side
of the school I could hear the voices of the children following Martin.

"I think you're all right," I said.

"Don't comfort me. *I don't want to be comforted.*"

"Tell me what happened next."

"I don't know why I should tell you anything. It's just
that you haven't understood Esther."

I kept my mouth shut, for once.

"You see, I knew you'd had a row as soon as she got
back. I knew you'd probably upset her as much as you'd
upset yourself. More, in fact—"

"She wasn't even bothered," I said. "She just sailed out.
She seemed rather grand."

"She didn't feel grand, of course. She'd come from a
country that frightened her. She hoped to find things as
she remembered them at Dartington."

I stared at my shoes. Perhaps I was Genghis Khan. I said,
"She was just so beautiful. . . ."

119

Trudi took a long shuddering breath. "So for that reason you tormented her."

"Yes . . . no . . . well . . ."

The racket was building up again at the corner as Martin came back toward us. God, how many morons had joined him now? I tried to ignore it and listened instead to Trudi's sniffs.

"I picked on her a bit," I said, "because I felt such a mess."

Where the path came into view I could now see most of the younger children. They were running forward and glancing behind them. Then came Martin, at three times their height. Following more slowly was another group, which now included children from the senior houses.

Trudi was sickened. "He's not even drawing attention to something. He's just going around. You'd better tell Esther that you're sorry. . . ."

I wasn't really looking, but I could see that Esther had joined the party at the back. My eyes picked her out as soon as she came in sight. She was calm, and when she saw me she spoke distantly, as if she hardly remembered me.

"Isn't it wonderful? So high in the air!"

"Bloody wonderful," I said.

She smiled and nodded like a film star; then she went down the hill behind the tall, strutting figure of Martin.

Personally, I thought Martin looked an absolute fool, and it didn't surprise me when his walk ended at the bottom of the hill, where the stilts went like scissors and Martin fell in the middle. Every one said, "Oh dear!" I took the steps down to the lane and climbed the hill toward the Hall. To hell with Martin. Esther could pick him up if she thought him so wonderful.

I went into the gardens. A winter sunshine was falling through the trees and lying on the terraced lawns. I walked all around the garden, looking at this and that, until I came to the arbor on the far side of the tiltyard, where I sat in the cold and watched the cloud shadows crossing the lawns. There was movement here and there: a gardener with a wheelbarrow passed behind the trees, and way over toward the church I saw a tall, barely moving figure with a basket who was probably Mrs. Elmhirst. She vanished like a ghost.

Now there was no one in the garden but me and a lot of sparrows. The sun came out again, lighting the great amphitheater where, so we were told, the knights had once ridden.

No one in the garden? A path bordered the tiltyard on the far side, and from there I saw a spark of color, made by a girl in red. A girl with a lame companion. I watched them as, again and again, they came into sight where the path was close to the lawns. She kept turning to him, no doubt saying how sorry she was about his fall and his bruises, and I thought they were holding hands. I watched the girl's lovely swishing walk and how the red skirt swirled around her legs.

I went away to the river, which ran below the garden. It was full and torn by currents. I found a place where a willow grew across the water, at the point of falling in, and holding this I leaned farther and farther out until I could see my head and shoulders reflected in the dark river below me. I was surprised to find that I looked quite ordinary.

I stayed there some time, my eyes following the drift of the water. I remember that a cold wind snaked around my ankles and that on the other bank were patches of blue frost. I thought about nothing much. I was lulled by the flow of the water until I didn't know if I was above the river or drifting about near the bottom. Either way, it didn't matter. The voice behind me must have spoken several times before I heard it.

I turned and my eyes came slowly into focus. The lady was tall and her head was bent to one side. Her mouth had turned into a little oval, as if she meant to whistle, but I couldn't imagine Mrs. Elmhirst doing that.

"I was just looking at the river," I said.

"Of course. The flow of water is so compelling." She walked slowly along the bank and I followed her. "I saw you from the garden. It looked so charming by the river I thought I would join you."

"I wasn't doing anything in particular."

"Why, no! Sometimes it is nice to stand still and let your mind glide away."

She didn't hurry, but she didn't stop, either. She led me away from the willow.

"You were thinking, perhaps? You were thinking of music?"

"Not really."

"Mind you, there are dangers in reflection. One's mind can become enclosed in darkness." I suppose, from anybody else, that would have sounded silly, but when spoken in an American voice, with a sort of purring sound before and afterward, it was quite impressive.

We continued down the path, getting farther away from the willow.

"Soon, Daniel, you must come to the Hall," Mrs. Elmhirst said. "My husband and I are anxious to hear your music, which they tell me is beautiful."

"I don't think it's beautiful."

She couldn't have listened. She went sailing on. She told

me of the musicians she would bring to the great hall for a concert of my music. We reached a gate that would take us back on to the drive.

"I may not come to the Hall," I said. "I'm sorry. I know how much you've done for me."

This time she heard me and her eyes swung round. She looked at me for a long time. "I believe you will, Daniel."

"Sometimes . . . sometimes I just don't feel like it."

Mrs. Elmhirst folded her arms on top of the gate and bent her head over them, as if I'd said something that needed a lot of deep thought. "You have a gift, Daniel, that must be served."

"It goes away sometimes."

"A gift always returns."

"It does?"

She bowed her head solemnly, telling me it was true. We went through the gate and she turned in the direction of the Hall, but I stayed where I was. I'd been hit by another black spell.

She took a pace up the long hill, and turned. "Just now there was a girl in the garden. A girl with lovely dark eyes."

I said, "I know."

"She was alone."

(Oh, how did she do it?)

She gave that faraway smile, and then went into a long "Mmmm . . ." that I thought would never stop.

"Alone?" I asked.

She nodded, the smile got larger, and I had the impression that nothing in her life—and she'd known kings and presidents, they said—had given her so much pleasure as telling me that Esther was alone in the garden.

"She had left her companion near the old churchyard. Poor boy, he seemed to have many bruises! She had con-

123

tinued on her own. I cannot say what she was doing, but I think she was looking for someone. Good-bye, Daniel!"

That night there was dancing. At the assembly hall the light was pouring from the door and I heard the gramophone playing inside. Benny Goodman, I think it was. I stayed in the shadows of the covered walk, watching the door, seeing how the light was broken again and again as the dancers went round inside. A shadow passed, and a pale face turned toward me like a question mark. Walter, of course. Walter in heavy boots. He paused at the door before going in. Between the dances I heard voices from the hall and sometimes laughter.

Then the doors crashed open behind me and I fell back into the dark. Martin appeared, propped up by two friends and a crutch. He didn't really need the crutch. They made a slow journey to the hall, Martin catching his breath at every step, and there was a cheer when he went in. How loud it sounded, even out here in the darkness!

I wandered away. I went on to the empty terrace, where the music conjured up imaginary dancers and I turned once or twice myself. I forget what else I did, but I know for certain that later I was back near the open door, and Esther was walking toward me. Her face was covered by the shadows, but the stiffness of her walk and the way her hands rested on her hips told me that she was angry.

"Why are you hiding out here? There's really no point."

"I like it here." I turned to the music.

"Everyone's inside, even Martin. What's happened to you since I went away?"

I stopped dancing. I thought I might cry. "I just wanted you to come back. More than anything."

"Well, I'm *back*."

124

Her figure, which I could see only in outline, was stiff and disapproving.

"Who told you I was here?" I asked.

"Walter," she said.

She moved away from me, shaking her head—I was a monster, of course—and I thought she'd go back into the hall. But she stayed there in the gloom, quite still, and it was only when I said her name that she moved, but slowly now, lifting her hands as if to say, "God, what a moron!" She came toward me without a sound and stopped just inches away, her breath playing over my cheek but so gently I barely felt it.

Then I heard the laughter rustle on her lips. "You really are an awfully silly boy," she said.

That was the first time I danced with Esther. She danced much better than I did and she didn't let me tread on her at all. Her eyes were full of warnings, but now and again I felt a tightening of her hands, as if she wanted to keep me there, and the flow of her hair against my cheek.

Now I could see nothing beyond Esther's face. The others had gone into a spinning fog. The music went on and on and Esther didn't go away. She stayed with me for ten minutes, for twenty. She wouldn't leave me! I heard a cheer, and I knew that Martin was dancing with Bella and the crutch combined. Let them cheer him, if they wanted. Good old Martin! I was only aware of Esther's cheek, of the lips that were nearly smiling, and of the whirling room beyond.

❧13❧

FOR A WHILE IN THAT SPRING AND SUMMER OF 1939, everything went right for Esther and me. Each day we were out by the Dart or the Bidwell. It was only later that things went wrong.

I'd better start with the morning Bolski set me to work on the longest piece I had so far attempted. It was sometime in March. I remember that he was late and that I fretted in the music room with nothing to do. I wanted to go but didn't quite. I went into the passage, as the first stage of going altogether, and stood by the window opposite the practice rooms. Outside, a tattered rook was flying above the trees, blown about by the wind. I was the only person alive at Dartington. Just me and a single rook.

But then, from one of the practice rooms, I heard a note struck once. It trailed a long echo in the empty corridor.

126

I went from one practice room to another. In the third I found Walter, the village boy, standing by the piano with one finger held over the keyboard. On the music rest was a sheet of manuscript I recognized as mine.

"All those notes, Danny."

"That piece isn't any good. I threw it away."

He was staring at the music, though I knew he couldn't read it. His large finger with a black and broken nail moved slowly up and down, searching for the opening note.

"It goes like this," I said, and played the first bars with one hand.

It meant nothing to him and his face remained blank. His eyes were dull and smudgy but they kept peering at the manuscript as if, bit by bit, he could make it out.

"Does she like music, Danny?"

"Who?"

He didn't say, but I knew he meant Esther.

"I never learned to play," Walter said. "Never saw a piano until I came here."

"It can be boring," I said.

"But she likes it, doesn't she? She likes music?"

I felt uneasy. He was thinking about Esther. "I don't know who you mean," I said.

Walter went out, followed by a bootlace, and at the same moment I heard Bolski's footsteps in the passage outside. I joined him in the music room. He was pale and out of breath.

"Forgive me, Daniel! There was much talk at the Hall. Much earnest talk among the refugees. You see, a war has become more likely and they risk internment."

"More likely?" I was still thinking about Walter and Esther and not about the war.

"Britain has given a pledge to Poland, which is a challenge to Hitler. I must believe it will lead to war. Dear me, I should not be troubling you with these things. We will sit down. We will resume our study."

"I hope you are not interned," I said. "It wouldn't be fair."

"In wartime there is little that is fair."

I said slowly, "If there's a war, I suppose we will win."

"My dear boy, I do not know! I am a professor of music. But I have seen the power of Germany and her dark cruelty. I have seen the madness of her leader. Yes, maybe you will win, but the war can only be terrible." He seated himself at the piano and threw up the lid. "We will get on. We have not much time. I want you to undertake a sustained work. Now. *At once.*"

"D'you think I can do it? You didn't think much of my last piece."

"You can do it. You *must.* You have, perhaps, the summer. After that I may not be able to help you."

"Gosh."

"I suggest a suite for strings. As yet, you have not the experience to handle the wind instruments, but you will find that strings alone give you adequate expression. You must work hard."

"I'll try."

"Hard, hard! As Schultz did when he was a boy. Enough of this Dartington. I will show you no mercy."

Though he shook with emotion, he wasn't very frightening. I just nodded.

"Then I bring together the musicians to play what you have written. They will expect a mature work."

There was nothing I could say to that, so I just sat beside him, silently, looking at the blank manuscript paper he'd put in front of me, hoping I could do it.

"I can't do more," he said. "Dear Daniel, I can't do more. . . ."

Then it was nearly summer. It showed in the woods, where the leaves were coming out, and in the open windows at Foxhole. The river fell, and grass grew thick along the banks, and at the foot of the hill the Bidwell ran sparkling over stones. It was by the Bidwell, one Sunday morning, that Esther, unusually, touched me of her own accord.

She was trailing a finger in the water. She wouldn't look at me. She was hiding behind her lashes. She wouldn't even admit that I was there, thrashing around beside her, wanting her to talk, to glance in my direction. She was smiling at something in the Bidwell. Her lips were small and round and beautifully red. (Of course, she was smiling at me, really, because she knew I was frustrated. She was doing the all-woman bit.)

All right, I thought, I would be offhand and far away and not really care. I rolled onto my back and watched the clouds passing overhead. And I kept it up for some minutes, following the clouds as they passed over the trees, singing a little. But I couldn't stay that way. Finally I turned back to her, stupidly, and watched the side of her face where the sunlight, mirrored by the water, made flickering patterns.

At last she spoke without turning toward me. "Soon there'll be a war, going on for years."

"No!" I said.

She nodded solemnly. "All the big cities will be destroyed, no brick standing on another." (Actually a lot of people were saying that at the time.)

"I don't believe it."

She saw no need for an answer. She had a secret. A dark,

129

frightful secret. "It will start very soon, with a rain of bombs from the sky. Most likely Dartington will be blown to pieces on the first day, being so revolutionary."

"Even this spot where we're sitting?"

Now she turned to me, looking scared.

"Perhaps," I said, "perhaps there's a bomb coming down now, at a thousand miles an hour, straight for this spot."

Her mouth flew open, and she raised a hand to cover it.

"We've got ten seconds to live. Nine, eight—"

"Don't be silly," Esther said. But she had lifted her shoulders from the grass, all the same.

"—seven . . ."

Her eyes were frightened. She took my hand, her fingers shaking. She looked at me with enormous eyes, asking me to say it wasn't true, bringing her body closer to mine, drawing my hand toward her small round breast in a movement that seemed continuous but never came to an end.

I was sorry, then. She wasn't as tough as she pretended. I was a callous ox who had no business saying such things to a refugee. I was watching her face so closely it became no more than a blur of light and shadow. She came nearer. Her forehead was so close to mine that, for a minute, I knew what was in her mind. The message had jumped between us. She was thinking of smoke and flame and buildings falling. She was holding on to me as she might have held on to the last man on earth. Our lips were almost touching, but not quite, because something was in the way, like a wall, and I knew that even if I used all my strength I couldn't break through it.

I shook myself awake and said, "It's not true—not really."

"I didn't think it was," Esther said.

130

I listened to the noise of the stream and to the calling of the rooks higher up the hill.

Then Esther rolled over and pushed me away from her. "You're a bit of an idiot, aren't you?"

Swallows were playing over the Bidwell, here and there marking the water. We lazed about on the grass until, much later, a sound in the wood above made us both sit up.

Someone was there. A twig snapped, I think. I looked up the hill, where the trunks grew close together, and I saw a white face that quickly disappeared. A figure was moving away, going still higher. He was almost hidden by the trees but once or twice I caught sight of him where the leaves thinned out. A stooping figure, dragging heavy feet. Walter.

Esther and I got up and climbed into the wood by the path.

"What's wrong with Walter?" I asked. Far off, I saw his pale face turn toward us in a long final glance. Esther waved to him. "What d'you do that for? He's not a friend."

"It doesn't matter."

I lagged behind her, watching the way her legs swerved through the undergrowth, gracefully. Her skirt and bottom were really very nice. I was still bothered about Walter.

She came to a gate, and there she waited. "He sends me notes. Quite often."

"Damn rotten awful stinking Walter," I said, standing three yards off.

"It doesn't do me any harm."

"Love notes, of course."

"I suppose so. They're not very well written."

"Damn rotten awful—"

"Don't go on, please! He can write to me if he wants to."

131

She was looking across the gate into a field where the grass was shining. Notes at Dartington, which passed this way and that, were usually declarations of love. My great brain had got to it at last: *Walter was in love with Esther.*

"Jolly cheek," I said.

I watched her from the corner of my eye, seeing the elegance of her sweater and the slim roundness of her body underneath. I didn't like the thought of Walter loving Esther. The idea left me with a hole in my head where cold winds were getting in. After a time, very slowly, I turned part of the way toward her, and a moment later she did the same. Our eyes met, and at once I snatched mine away, after which Esther laughed and blew a little jet of air at the point of my chin. She was telling me not to fuss about Walter.

Then I just stood there, looking at her, trapped by the brown darkness of her eyes where my own face was reflected. I couldn't look away. I'd have done anything she wanted, like jump in the river. The sun lay in the grass beyond the gate, and children were playing there, but I paid them no attention. For a long time I was aware of nothing but the rise and fall of her breast and of the fiery glow way back in her eyes.

By midsummer I had my suite for strings nearly finished. It contained five short movements, each with something like a dance rhythm. These were bound together by an open melody which was repeated in variation until it crashed out in dominant form at the close. (Daniel, the great composer!) I think Bolski was startled by the finale— certainly he lost his spectacles when he played it—but he didn't say it was bad. In fact, he told me the thematic material was a matter for me alone and it was only the detailed scoring that he criticized.

"Think, Daniel! This phrase, it cannot be played upon a bowed instrument. The left hand has not the reach. Have I taught you nothing in two years?"

He would jump up and down on the piano stool. But then he would grow calm and play from my score himself, moving his head, sometimes in little jerks, sometimes in great circles, until he came to a natural close. "It becomes a beautiful work, Daniel. I am too harsh with you. You will write with greater maturity, but never, I think, will you find a fresher melody, nor describe the subject with such fullness of heart. . . . Yes, there is a subject! This is not a suite but a serenade. She is there in each phrase, each loveliness. . . . But I say no more! In these matters the master has no right to intrude. You have still much to do in part scoring."

On the afternoon of Midsummer Day (I know the day, because we planned a ghost walk that night), I found Bolski sitting at the piano, sniffing and wiping his nose.

After a while, he said, "Our time is shortened still further, Daniel. They have got together, Hitler and his bloated assistant, Mussolini. Germany and Italy in a Pact of Steel. Can you imagine a greater blasphemy?"

Often he spoke like that, without expecting an answer. He ran his eyes over the manuscript and nodded with approval at the changes I had made.

"It is better—better. Maybe it is enough."

"Can it be played, d'you think?"

"Yes, it can be played."

"It won't do if it isn't good enough."

He squeezed his forehead between his thumb and first

finger. He was getting fed up with Daniel, the composer. "It will be played at the summer concert. I am bringing together the estate musicians and will myself direct. A small thing to set beside the martyrdom of Europe. . . ."

I should have been pleased, but I wasn't. "I'd like to rewrite the finale."

"It is too late." But a moment later he raised his head. "Dear boy, I have disappointed you. You have achieved something of beauty. This piece, which to spare your blushes we will call the 'Dartington Serenade,' has the charm of discovery, of a mind awakening to a world of loveliness. It has given me hope and courage."

"I see," I said. "Thank you."

"It could only have been written by a young man of sixteen with a bountiful gift."

"Thank you very much."

I went out, but in the hall I turned in a circle and came back, finding Bolski still sitting at the piano. "I mean, I really am grateful—for your putting up with me, and all that."

His shoulders rocked like a seesaw. "It is nothing," he said. "I could have done nothing else."

Ghosts. Ghosts in the moonlight. Now on Midsummer Night we were going to seek them out. There was a ghost in North Wood, just as there was one in the Hall garden. I had seen the white lady in the tiltyard more than once, but each time it turned out to be Martin (or somebody) under a sheet. In fact, it was quite *usual* to see a ghost gliding along the terraces and disappearing with a howl into the bushes. However, I'd never seen the headless huntsman who was said to haunt the paths of North Wood and a nearby hillside where there was an old stone ruin called Hunter's Lodge. Martin claimed to have seen him, but Martin would.

We stole out after eleven o'clock and no one heard us: Martin and Bella (who were now in love), Trudi, Esther and me. Our whispers were thin in the cold air. The moon hung large over the distant woods as we went down the lane toward the Old Postern. At one moment I heard a footstep behind us—the clump of a heavy boot on the hard road—and looking back I saw a figure in the lane.

Walter was following at a distance. Walter, who was in love with Esther. How did he know?

We quickened our pace, and Walter stopped. He stayed where he was in the middle of the lane as we hurried away. His face, which was pale and watchful, faded out until we could no longer see it. Silly old Walter, we said.

We followed a rutted track, where haystacks showed white in the moonlight.

"The huntsman carries a deadly weapon," Martin said. "He'll cut you to pieces and leave you on the path."

Bella snorted, but she kept pace with Martin, holding his arm. Trudi, who didn't believe in ghosts, lagged behind, saying she couldn't walk so fast. Esther was silent beside me.

"Just gibbering guts," said Martin.

The moonlight shone on the face of North Wood, showing the covering of leaves, but under the branches there were hollows of darkness where, if you tried, you could imagine a capering ghost. So far, I wasn't frightened at all and only the thought of Walter somewhere in the darkness bothered me. I turned my head. I listened, but I couldn't hear him. Once I saw a figure against the white of the hayricks, but that may have been imagination as well.

"It is foolish, of course, this ghost," Trudi said.

135

We took a path that led under the trees. Here the branches cut out the moon and we looked back to the meadow, where the light still shone. The trees loomed darkly beside us. We jumped all over the place when a rabbit scuttled away. I felt the soft touch of Esther's hand on my arm and the brush of her hair along my shoulder. I wanted to put my arm around her waist, but I didn't dare. I just kept her hand pressed to my side and felt the warm nearness of her cheek.

Bella stumbled and fell, making a lot of noise, but Esther and I stayed together, ignoring Bella, paying no attention when Martin said the huntsman had got her with one blow of his sword; we were moving up the path as if they were not there. For a minute or two (no longer, because there was something around the corner) we were alone together in the dark, touching, her face caught once in a while by a gleam of moonlight.

It didn't last. Where the path climbed toward the top of the hill, where the trees grew thin, we saw the huntsman. He was standing in a pool of moonlight at a distance of a dozen yards. Erect, he seemed, a bright weapon held high up, a shadow where his head should have been.

We stopped in terror. Only Trudi wandered on toward the huntsman.

"Come back!" we called. *"He'll get you!"*

But Trudi didn't stop. Some time ago she'd been treated by an analyst in Berlin, and she saw things differently from us. Her fantasies had been wiped away. There weren't any ghosts, only illusions. We watched in silence as she ambled toward the huntsman, expecting I don't know what. And we watched again as she went beyond him to get lost in the dark.

"It's only a sack in a tree," Trudi called from higher up the path.

All right. A sack in a tree. We laughed as we went up the hill behind Trudi. There were no ghosts at Dartington, of course; our minds had been freed from superstition. The ghosts had gone a mile away to flutter in the gloom like wounded bats. Now there was dew under the trees which rubbed my cheeks. We crossed North Wood until we could hear the river below.

Hunter's Lodge was on a nearby hill, at the foot of which the dew had thickened into a mist. Above the mist the trees showed again, rising to a summit where we could just see the ruined lodge on the skyline. The moon was catching it now and gleaming on the gray stone. We climbed the hill to the lodge, breaking into a run as we covered the last yards.

"There's nothing here," Bella said. "Just broken walls."

"Wait—listen!" said Martin.

We sat on the crumbling step, giving the ghost a chance, while the moonlight shimmered inside the roofless building and out. Below us a little valley reached toward the Old Postern, where, far away now, the hayricks were just visible. North Wood lay like a whale on our right. Once, a dog barked, but nowhere near. A star fell in the distance.

Trudi said it was cold. "I don't know why we sit here when nothing will appear. I give no importance to immaterial things."

"Go back, then," Martin said.

"So I will!"

She got up with an angry hiss and went down the hill. It was a long time before she came back into our sight, and then she was no bigger than a beetle—a small black beetle stumping down the valley path. Nothing much happened after that. Once, Martin went behind the lodge and made a gurgling sound, but he was so obvious we took no notice. Slowly the moon swung across the sky. Midnight came, but though we strained our ears for a footstep or a clank of metal, there was nothing but silence.

"He didn't come," Bella said. She wanted someone to blame and Martin was the obvious choice. "At least you could've *arranged* a ghost."

They had a fight on the far side of the lodge. We heard the sound of their bodies rolling about in the grass. I don't know how it ended, but later we saw them arm-in-arm on the lower slope of the hill. They didn't say good-bye, they just vanished into the trees.

Now Esther and I were alone at the lodge, seated side by side, not touching. I wanted to hold her, but I hadn't the courage. I was waiting, I suppose, for someone else to start it—perhaps Esther, perhaps the huntsman, perhaps a winged spirit floating over the lodge.

"Professor Bolski says the serenade is very good," Esther said, but she kept her eyes on the valley.

"It's probably rotten."

"He played me some of it."

"He *did?*"

So Bolski and Esther had been together, playing my music. I said, "That was cheeky."

"It's lovely, Danny."

She turned toward me, and that nearly did it. I saw the solemn eyes and the small firm mouth. More than anything I wanted her to like the serenade. Her eyes stayed on my face. She laughed softly. I knew only that she and I were alone on the hillside, together with the moon and whatever ghosts were still around.

Then she lifted her head, rolling it back until her lips were close to mine. She put a hand on my arm, setting me free. I remember that I held her for a long time, my lips within an inch of hers, watching the way her eyelids fell slowly across the moon's reflection. I remember the first touch of her lips, which were cold and moistened by dew, and the long, firm, rocking kiss that seemed to go on forever.

In a minute, perhaps, she fell away from me, her eyes open, her lips parted.

"Esther," I said. "Esther."

"Thanks, Danny," she said. She took hold of my collar and pulled me toward her until she could whisper in my ear. "Thank you for everything. Thank you for being there. At least something was the same."

We had nothing more to say. We laughed and shuffled our feet. We had become ordinary, and we would have stayed that way but for something that happened at the same moment and set my heart beating again.

We heard a noise at the end of the valley. Not speaking, just wailing. We sprang up.

"What is it?" Esther asked, alarmed.

Then a bright flame leaped up from the fields down by the farm—a rose-red flame that grew higher as we watched. God, *we'd started a fire!* I held Esther close to me, and I could not have said if I was comforting her or myself. We saw a second flame spring up close to the first. The glow spread into the fields and lit up the face of North Wood. We heard the crackle of the fire, which reached us even at the end of the dark valley.

We spoke together. "Walter!" we said.

No doubt about it. Walter had set fire to the hayricks. He knew, *he knew*. There was nothing we could do but watch the flames. They rose to a great height, with tongues of flame reaching the lower sky, before sinking down to an angry red.

"Gosh," we said. "Oh, *gosh!*"

❧ 14 ❧

I NEVER KNEW FOR CERTAIN WHAT HAPPENED to Walter after he burned the ricks. He didn't come back to school. Someone said that his father, the gardener, had beaten him until he cried for mercy, forgetting Dartington's principles, and this may have been true. I saw him only once, a few weeks later. He was pruning shrubs in the Hall garden and he didn't speak to me, or look around, though he knew I was there.

At about this time Professor Bolski began to rehearse the *Dartington Serenade* with the estate musicians. These were students from the music school helped out by members of the staff. The concert would be given in the great hall in the last week before the holiday. I got jumpy about this; I thought Bolski was making too much of the serenade, which wasn't *that* good, but he kept telling me it was fine. "If God is kind to me, Daniel, I will one day attend a concert of your mature music. I sit only in the back row. I hear the applause. I content myself with the thought that it was I who taught you the elements of form."

(Well, that's what he *said*. I'm not making it up.)

I went to the first rehearsal in the great hall. I sat alone in the middle of the huge floor and felt rather silly. All this had nothing to do with me, it seemed, because Bolski was speaking to the musicians in a language I couldn't understand. The prelude sounded unlike anything I had written. The score had been taken away from me by strangers and made into something different. God, it's terrible, I thought. Later there were passages I recognized, but now the melodies seemed dull and obvious, and I'd have told them to stop, to play something else, if I could've found the courage. I sat there, unable to move, wishing it over, listening to a blur of sound that seemed to go on forever. In my head I was adding a new line in the bass: "*Bloody . . . rotten . . . awful . . . stinking. . . .*"

It wasn't much better when, at the end, Bolski turned toward me, his baton under his arm, and clapped. He was keeping my spirits up, of course. I ran out of the hall and down to the river, where Esther had promised to meet me.

It was better there. She lay beside me, holding me. Her hair was a black cloud just in front of my eyes. When her lips pressed mine they were soft and rather eager. Behind her, I could see a tall clump of grass with vetch and speedwell mixed inside. A patch of cow parsley was hiding us from the Marsh from where, sometimes, we could hear voices passing.

I must have held her for an hour, until my arms were tired, and then I laid her in the grass and looked at her through half-shut eyes, seeing the way her chin rose slowly as she brought her lips closer to mine. (Imagine that! Esther was asking *me*.) She took my arms and wrapped them around her waist, as she might have wound herself in a blanket.

Then I held her again, pressing my lips into her neck, feeling her soft arms creep up to my shoulders and then hold me in a clasp even stronger than mine. She said, more than once, "Don't let me go, Danny." My ears sang, blotting out the voices from the Marsh.

When I lifted my head again, and the sun shone into my eyes, I saw that she was smiling. I ran my fingers along her lips and cheek, fixing the smile, just as it was. I wanted her to look like that forever. When the smile wavered I pushed her cheeks upward to bring it back. I brought my lips into the hollow of her ear and told her she was beautiful. I'd never told her before, if you can believe it! She didn't exactly nod, but she didn't tell me it was rubbish, either.

Her eyes followed the birds as they circled overhead or dived down toward the river. Of course, I knew why she was smiling. She was beautiful, her skirt made a lovely swirl on the grass, and she'd only to flash her eyes and I'd do cartwheels along the Marsh. And there was nothing that could take these things away from her just then.

A minute later there were voices on the river, and the splash of a paddle, and a canoe drifted into our sight. It was moving with the current toward Folly Island. The occupants were dressed in colored shirts, and one wore a white cap with a peak: Marcelline and Royden Clancy. They were reflected exactly in the surface of the river. We lay in the grass, almost covered by a tuft of rushes on the river side, and let them pass. We could hear the splash of the paddle for a long time after they went behind the island.

143

Now we were bursting with laughter. Everyone had come down to the river today, but no one had seen us yet! I put my arms around her again. We rolled over and over, until she lay above me with her hair falling on either side of her face like a tent.

"Stay with me, Danny," she said. "Don't go away."

The day kept warm. At tea time we were the only people left beside the Dart. We got up from the battered grass and walked toward Foxhole. We walked hand in hand, our arms swinging, her fingers locked around mine so that I couldn't let her go. She was hanging on to me, to the river, to Dartington.

At length she said, "Royden and Marcelline are going back to California. They won't be here next term."

"What are they going for?"

"Oh—the war. Others are leaving, too."

We didn't mention it again. We didn't dare. You see, everything was packed into those two hours at Folly Island, and after that everything went wrong.

❦ 15 ❧

I TRIED TO FORGET ABOUT THE CONCERT, BUT
I couldn't do that forever. For one thing, when the day
came, just about the whole school decided to attend, and
of course I got into a state. When Esther and I left for the
Hall, we could see a line of children climbing High Cross
Hill and disappearing over the top. I don't know what they
expected: a disaster, probably. There was still a glimmer of
sunlight when we came to the gardens, where there were
people on all the paths and I could hear their excited
voices. I stopped at the arbor.

"I hadn't realized there'd be so many people."

"They've been talking about it for weeks," Esther said.
"The ballet, the Chekov School. Everybody."

"It's only a piece of music."

We sat in the arbor and watched the people, near and far off, walking toward the Hall.

"I don't want to go."

She took my hand and held it tightly between hers. She said, "You've got to go. It means so much to them, with the war coming, and all that."

"You'll sit with me, then? And you won't go away when it's over?"

"If that's what you want."

I had something more to say. I moved our hands, so that now I was holding hers and pressing them between mine. "I mean, you won't go away *at all.*"

She raised her head, and even in the soft light of the arbor I could see her pale cheek and trembling lips. She said, "I can't make promises."

Still they were coming through the garden. I saw Bella and Martin and the rest of my group on the far side of the tiltyard. Esther was quiet; then she kissed the palm of her hand and patted my cheek with it.

"We'd better go now. It's getting late."

"I'd rather stay here."

"But I've promised . . ."

"What? *Who?*"

She said, "I promised Professor Bolski I'd get you there. He knows how emotional you can be."

"I'll kill Bolski."

When I stood up, Esther straightened my tie, pulling my head this way and that. "You *do* look a mess," she said.

Now there were fewer people in the garden. I heard footsteps here and there but most of them had gone beyond us. We went by the rose walk and came into the courtyard in time to see the last of the audience going in under the tower.

146

"God," I said. "I don't think—"

"Just shut up." Esther was holding my arm and pushing me forward like a bicycle. "Just shut up altogether."

Professor Bolski was standing on the porch with Mrs. Elmhirst and her husband, Leonard. From inside the hall I could hear a great many voices. When he saw me, the professor took my hand and pressed it. "So much is owed to you, Daniel. So much!"

"Indeed, that is true," said Leonard Elmhirst.

I couldn't let go of Bolski's hand. I swung it around, trying to find something to say but not finding it, while my eyes became hot and I thought I might cry.

"We start with the Bach," Bolski said.

"Bach."

"The serenade will of course be the final work."

"Work."

He kissed Esther's hand, which she didn't mind too much. Mrs. Elmhirst had gone into one of her trances. "Oh, that Joachim Schultz could have been here!" she said.

When I entered the great hall between Esther and Mrs. Elmhirst, there was a murmur of interest that put me right off. I was aware of a lot of faces turned toward me like peeled potatoes. The school was mainly in the gallery at the back of the hall and when they saw me they hooted and stamped and cheered, but I took no notice. I marched straight ahead, going faster and faster until Esther was running to keep up with me.

We were seated in the front row under the platform. I leaned against Esther and watched the musicians filing in from the private door.

"It's a mistake," I said. "It was meant for you. Just *you*."

147

But Esther only ran her fingers over my hand, saying, "Sssh!"

I can't remember the Bach violin concerto except that it was loudly applauded. I banged my hands together like cymbals. I know that in the interval I walked on the terrace with the Elmhirsts and listened to a long dirge about "music as an aid to social harmony." Some of the audience had wandered into the garden and I saw their colors on the lawns. Back in the hall, I sat with my head between my knees. Esther tried to prod me upright but I was too far gone to do anything. I heard the audience going back to their seats and the musicians returning to the platform.

I hoped there'd be no introduction, but after a while the voices became quiet, there were footsteps on the platform, and I knew that some moron was going to make a speech.

"Friends of Dartington. . . ." Oh, how well mannered the voice was, how superior! Leonard Elmhirst, of course. "There is little I can say about the final work that will not be obvious to you. . . ." He went on with a lot more stuff of which I caught snatches here and there: ". . . time of darkness and despair . . . man's capacity for wrongdoing . . . may ask if it's still possible to hope. . . ."

Before he came to an end, Esther bent toward me and spoke in a whisper. "Listen!" she said, and I jumped up, as if shot.

"Well, I suggest that hope can still be entertained," Leonard Elmhirst was saying, "and a brighter future foreseen, when we listen to the music our young composer has given us; for here you will find the qualities that these days so notably lack." He went on to thank Professor Bolski for teaching me and to say something about Joachim Schultz,

148

who had put me to work a few months before his death in Spain. He called him a European Martyr "whose spirit would live on in the works of his young contemporary." (*Me*, you understand.)

During the applause, I sank back into the chair, wondering how it had happened. They were making too much of it, of course. All because of the war. . . . I watched Bolski raising his baton to begin the serenade.

Today, weeks later, I don't remember the performance very well. It seems to have taken place years ago. As the piece was not recorded, and I've no idea what happened to the score after I left Dartington, the music vanished as soon as it was played. It may have been awful, and the fuss they made of it no more than a last fling before the war began.

I remember how my eyes kept going back to the huge beams above my head, and how I followed them from one side to the other. When I glanced at the audience, I saw how serious they looked, no doubt supposing they mustn't look anything but serious. I watched the daylight fading behind the arched windows, and then, when my eyes had nothing else to do, I watched the two buttons on the back of Bolski's coat that bounced and swayed in a small, separate performance. Once I caught sight of Mr. Curry in the row behind me. His hands were clasped over his knee, his head was bent forward, his concentration was so great he had blotted out the people on either side of him.

Esther was still there, sitting next to me, but when I took her hand I found it cold and lifeless. I pressed my fingers between hers, trying to catch her eye, but she replied with just a ghostly touch. I moved our hands in time with the music but she hardly joined in. She was sitting bolt up-right, her neck stiff, her head erect. She didn't blink, she didn't move.

She'd gone away without a word!

I shook her by the elbow, frightened, but though her head rocked she didn't turn to me. For a moment or two I believed that everything was going. Esther, the music, Dartington. I watched a tear gather in the corner of her eye, spill on to her cheek and run down toward her mouth.

"Esther," I said. "Esther, what is it?"

A moment later I was surprised by a storm of applause. It burst over my head and drummed in my ears. I saw Esther start up and applaud as eagerly as the others. I sank into the chair, crushed by the sound, my head falling lower and lower, my feet stretching across the floor.

Bolski was facing me now, clapping, urging me to stand, and behind him the musicians were clapping as well. Mrs. Elmhirst bent toward me, telling me that I must "acknowl-edge their applause," but now I was almost flat on the floor, rigid, stuck. It was Esther who got me to my feet. She took my hand and gave a great heave, like pulling a deck chair upright, and I found myself looking into the delighted face of Professor Bolski.

"Magnificent!" he said, shaking my hand. "It was indeed an inspiration."

Then, roughly, Esther turned me to face the audience and I heard a cheer from the hall.

"Bow," Esther hissed, and I bowed.

"Bravo! Bravo!" they shouted. "Oh, *bravo!*"

"What was it?" I asked, scared of the answer, as we made our way back through the dark gardens toward Foxhole. The other children had gone ahead until we could no longer hear them. "You went white, all of a sudden."

"I was frightened for a moment. That was all."

Then she told me she was going to Austria in August, as she'd done each year.

I had my arm around her waist, holding her tightly against my side. I didn't want her to go even a foot away.

"But you'll come back next term. We'll both be here at the end of September." I said it loudly, which made it sound true. "After all, we've got another year at Dartington."

"Yes, yes, I expect so," was all she said.

We came to a place where low branches made a deep shadow underneath, and here I stopped. I pulled her into this dark place.

"You can't want a lot more hugging at the moment," Esther said, using her practical voice. "Not after *all that.*"

"Oh, I *do.*"

She laughed—her ordinary laugh—and pressed her cheek against mine. Her eyes showed for a moment, catching some truant light, and they didn't seem worried.

"The music was lovely, Danny. I don't know how you did it."

"I just thought of you."

"That's silly. Really silly."

But she put her arms around my neck, all the same, and brought her lips gently against mine. She was so beautiful I nearly toppled over. I saw the edges of the leaves and some vague flowers beyond, but nothing else. And the garden was quiet—so quiet, I thought I could hear the beating of her heart, the brush of her lips against mine, the soft tumbling of her hair.

"Were you really thinking of me?"

"Oh, *yes.*"

151

She worked her chin into the hollow of my neck. "Thanks, Danny. It's nice to belong to somebody. It will make the next months easier."

We swayed together like dancers. Gradually I forgot how Esther had turned pale and frightened.

"Don't you want to go back to school?" she asked. "They're doing a late supper, with cider. You'll be the hero."

"I want to stay here "

"There'll be plenty more times."

"There will?"

"We'll come back to this spot, again and again. Just now, we have to go."

The only answer I could give was to hold her more tightly, refusing to move, while the warm air lapped my cheek and beyond these shadows, just visible in the starlight, there were any number of pale, vanishing blooms.

I woke suddenly from a deep sleep and raised myself on one arm. Why, I couldn't say. The window was still dark and there was no sound in the school. I could see Esther's face as I had seen it in the hall. White, at the point of leaving. For a time I believed that Esther had walked into my room, silently, her lips saying good-bye. I put out my hand to catch her, to prevent her from going, but I hit just the empty air. It was nothing, I said. I was just dreaming. It will be better in the morning.

I put on the light. Of course, the room was quite ordinary—nothing but a tennis racket, a pile of music, parts of a bicycle. It must have been a dream, because only in dreams did the worst things happen. Only in dreams did you lose everything. I wanted to see Esther, but it was still dark.

I got up and went into the corridor, in pajamas, just as I was. I heard nothing on the stair, nor was anyone about when I reached the courtyard, but the air had cooled and grown damp and there was a lightness in the sky over the roofs. I crossed to the junior houses.

I went on tiptoe to her room, where a band of gray light showed me the door was just open. Slowly I pushed it forward. Inside the window light fell on the bed and part of the floor. I could see her black hair spread across the pillow like a fan. I must have stumbled then, and crashed the door into the wall. She woke with a start.

"Who is it?"

"You're still there?" I asked. "You haven't gone away?"

"Of course I haven't gone away."

I heard the rattle of a matchbox and saw the leap of a flame. Esther was sitting up in bed and lighting a candle. (At Foxhole, we all had the means for reading after lights out.) She pulled the curtains closed.

"You're overexcited. It must have been the concert or the cider afterward."

"I was worried."

"There was no need."

I sat on her bed, the candle burning softly nearby. So far she hadn't smiled. The warm light lay on her shoulders, which the nightdress hardly hid at all, and at the sight of her, for a time, I went off the deep end again and was unable to speak.

"I think you must be a little mad," Esther said.

"You might have disappeared, you see. You might have gone somewhere without telling me."

"Well, I haven't. . . ."

"I just thought."

Her eyes became more friendly and she pulled her knees

153

up to her chin. "You *do* look stupid, sitting there."

"It was awful, for a time," I said. Even here in the glow of the candle the nightmare hadn't gone. "I don't want you to go to Austria. I want you to stay here."

"It's only for a few weeks. I'll be back at the end of September."

"Something may happen."

The flame trembled in a draft of air. Outside it was nearly dawn and a breeze was beginning. I was cold and frightened.

"I'll be all right," Esther said.

I nodded, telling myself it was true. I raised her hand to my cheek and felt the bed-warmth of her skin. Her body was slim and smooth and touched by shadows. I kissed her arm for a long time while her eyes sparkled in the candle-light.

"I don't know why you put up with me," I said.

"Neither do I."

"D'you think you will—next term—and after that?"

"I just might."

"Then . . ."

I tried not to think of the future. When I did, I went back to the nightmare, where Esther came to me in the dark-ness, saying good-bye. I sat on the edge of her bed, in a little ring of candlelight, with Esther so close I could feel her nearness even when I wasn't touching her. For a long time I watched the flame as it swayed and guttered.

But I couldn't make the minutes last forever. I looked again at Esther, and her face grew older as I watched. She became pale, and her eyes opened until they were enormous. It had been the same during the concert. She was looking at something I hadn't the courage to look at myself.

"Actually, we don't know what will happen," she said.

154

I must have grabbed her then. I remember how she fell backward on the bed, my face becoming smothered in her hair. I held her as closely as I could. She said "Steady on!" or something like that, but I was crying into her shoulder, calling her darling for the first time, turning my head this way and that as if her hair would wipe my tears.

"You can't go. You *can't.*"

She stroked the back of my head without speaking.

"I love you! I love you! *I love you!*" I said.

Still she didn't speak, but gently she sorted out the tangle of arms and bedclothes. Her nightdress had fallen from her shoulders, but nonetheless she held my head in her arms, letting my cheek rest upon her small firm breast, and in silence she rocked me to and fro.

❧16❧

LATER THAT MORNING, CURRY ASKED ME TO
come to his study. It was the last day of the term. "Sit
down, Daniel," Curry said. "Take a comfortable chair.
Last night was a great occasion for us all."

I should have guessed what was coming. He made a
basket of his fingers and looked into it. Under the desk his
little legs moved about awkwardly. I stared into the courtyard where the porters were bringing out the heavy luggage, and making a pile of it, before the summer holiday.

"Last week I received a letter from your father. You must
forgive me if I haven't told you about it until now. You see,
I thought it best not to disturb you before the concert."

"Yes?" I was still looking into the courtyard.

"Your father wishes you to join him in New York. I
understand your mother has given her consent in view

of the international situation and the danger to this country."

"Yes?"

"You will travel on the *Queen Mary* a few weeks from now. In the meantime, you will have the opportunity of seeing your mother in London."

With an effort I brought my eyes back from the window. "But I'll be coming back. This is only for the holiday. I'll be at Dartington next term."

Curry's knees shifted round again. "That is not so, I'm afraid. Your father speaks of an American school for the time being. There are, of course, some excellent schools available where you will be able to continue your musical training."

"I don't want to go."

"I'm afraid you have no choice. Needless to say, we'll be sorry to lose you."

"I'd rather stay here. I don't care about the war or being killed."

"It's your father's wish."

"He can't do this to me," I said, knowing that he could. "He hasn't seen me for three years. I'm not going."

"You'll have a chance to see America. Had you thought of that?"

"Damn America. Oh, *God.* . . ."

Curry was silent for a time, his eyes on the desk. "I know how you feel, Daniel. I know why you wish to stay here. You have made yourself a life at Dartington it will be hard to break. But, with time—"

"No!" I said.

"Daniel, Daniel. The war will make changes in all our lives. Esther herself may not return from Austria."

"Then why's she going?"

157

"I understand her parents have no alternative but to take Esther to their home in Vienna. Both have been deprived of their passports by the Nazi regime and Esther would be stranded in this country if war breaks out."

I said, "It's not as if our parents were really bothered. . . ." But I couldn't go on. I put my head into my hands. I was crying. "Surely Mrs. Elmhirst could adopt her or something?"

"That would not be possible, Daniel." I heard him get up and go to the window; he drew the curtains softly closed. "I want you to listen carefully. The separation from Esther will hurt you a great deal. I'm sure that your love for her is real and that it fills your life at present. But you are only sixteen and you cannot know how your life will develop. Esther is barely fifteen. You are at an age when there are few certainties, when a hurt may not be prolonged—"

"No!" I shouted. "You don't understand."

"Believe me, I am trying to."

"I love her."

"I have acknowledged that."

"It's not as you say. It's *not!*"

Curry went back to his place behind the desk. I could see that he didn't like doing this to me. After a time he said, "It would be cruel of me to insist that I am right. Possibly your love for Esther is final."

"Then what can you do?"

"I think, nothing."

"I want us to stay together."

"Of course you do. But I am not your guardian, only your headmaster. I must ask you to prepare yourself for a separation."

I suppose I cried again.

Curry said softly, "There may not be a war. You may see Esther again quite soon." But I could make nothing of that. They were taking her away.

"You will still have your music," Curry said.

"That's just—nothing."

"You will find pleasure in it again."

"No! No! *No!*"

"Daniel, whatever happens, I cannot believe that you will be heartbroken forever. All suffering is healed by time. Now I must ask you to put your things together. You would of course be unwise to leave anything at Dartington."

Ossi Nin helped me take my bicycle to pieces and put it in a box. I wasn't bothered about the music, but Professor Bolski made me collect my manuscripts and tie them in a bundle. I didn't say much when he told me I must continue my study, but I did manage to thank him (without actually crying) before he went away, carrying the manuscripts under his arm.

Later Bella and Martin called up to my window, to ask where I was going.

"New York," I said.

They both said, "Gosh!" Then Martin added, "I'm going to Scotland. Curry reckons half the school will have left in six months."

Trudi told me the same when she came to my room after lunch. "You'll be better off in New York. London will be flattened in the first week of war. Daniel—however much you don't want to—I would like you to kiss me."

I kissed her and she went out.

For most of the children it was just the last day of term. I could hear laughter and running footsteps.

In the afternoon I went to Esther's room, where I found

her packing a suitcase. Her clothes lying across the bed were like memories. At first she ignored me.

"I suppose you know about me," I said.

She nodded and went on with her packing, rather fiercely.

"I told Curry I didn't want to go, but it was no good."

"Of course not."

I wanted to walk, to leave Foxhole and the excited children, and in a little while Esther slammed the case shut and came with me. We went without speaking across the fields and down the hillside to the river. Not even the best part of the river—just the meadows beyond the lower drive, where the willows were old and falling into the water.

I tried to take her hand, but she kept it behind her back. We were wasting time, as I knew we would. Her face was white, her eyes dry and fixed. I remembered, then, that I'd never seen Esther cry except for a few tears during the concert, which didn't count. Always it was me, the big boo-hoo. Where the river bent toward the Marsh, we stopped by the stile, and here I sat down and threw pebbles into the water. She sat behind me where I couldn't see her. Now and again she made small sounds that told me she was still there, still my companion.

For an hour we sat on the riverbank, wasting time, while I listened to the rise and fall of her breath, on which I could hear the beginnings of a sob, or thought that I did. The drift of the river was slow. I watched a leaf that came into my sight beyond the reeds and saw how it was carried downstream to vanish in the light a hundred yards away.

"I'll see you again tomorrow morning," I said.

"There's no point."

"My train doesn't leave until ten."

Still her breath trembled, making a slight sound. "I'm

not going to cry. I absolutely won't," she said.

No, Esther mustn't cry. Tears were not allowed in her distant country. And, as it happened, my own eyes were dry as dust.

"I won't let anything make me cry," Esther went on. "Not anything."

"Let me kiss you, then."

"If you want."

I took her in my arms, but her body was stiff, her cheeks like paper, her lips as brittle as a leaf.

I said, "There may not be a war. We may both come back to Dartington."

"It won't be like that."

"We're wasting time."

"How can we? It's over. Yesterday was our last day."

"But you're still there," I said.

I don't know why those words should have done it. I hadn't meant to upset her. She sobbed once, twice, and then fell weeping on my neck. I put my arms around her and felt the hot tears on my cheek. We collapsed into the grass, each struggling for a tighter hold, rolling back and forth, crying.

"Danny, Danny, don't let me go!" Esther said.

We hugged each other until we were out of breath. Then, still holding her, I raised myself upon one elbow. I looked down the river where, because of my tears, the water and sky were like broken glass.

A long shadow, that of a tall person, was moving across the grass nearby. I looked up to see Mrs. Elmhirst passing behind me, walking as silently as she could. Then she realized that I had seen her.

"My dears, I'm sorry to have disturbed you. In fact, I didn't know you were there."

Her husband, Leonard, came toward us from the stile. Perhaps something in my face caught Mrs. Elmhirst's attention, for she stopped, her head on one side. (To tell the truth, my face must have looked like a traffic smash-up just then.)

"There is something wrong?"

I told her that I was going to America, Esther to Europe.

"That is so? Leonard, did you hear? These young people have separate journeys to make. Then, my dears, you must be patient for a while."

"I suppose so," I said.

"Only a while. The war can't last forever. Then it will be my pleasure to invite you back to Dartington. Both of you—*together.*"

I felt a little better. Mrs. Elmhirst had all the money in the world. It was stacked in vaults, pile upon pile. She had the magic of riches and she could make anything happen if she wanted to.

"After all," Mrs. Elmhirst said, "you can't be separated if you really don't want to be. And that's a fact."

"Of course not!" said Leonard Elmhirst, from behind her.

"Don't you forget, then, either of you. First thing after the war. . . ."

She smiled gracefully and continued her walk toward the drive.

Then we were alone. I looked at Esther and was surprised to find her smiling. Maybe she too was thinking of all those pots of money. She gazed into my face. She put out a hand and touched my cheek. She ran her fingers around the curve of my chin. She actually laughed, and drew me toward her, shaking her head to rub out everything we'd said

162

so far, keeping only the present, which wasn't as bad as we'd thought it.

All right, she was saying, we'll enjoy this afternoon, making it last, and then at some moment in the future we'll come back to Dartington.

My lips hovered over hers for a long time—how long, I could not have said, though I could just hear the flow of the Dart behind us, and how it seemed to run slower and slower, stretching the time. Her embrace was warm now and very close. I saw the light in her eyes that was slowly put out as the lids closed in amazement. For a long while I held her slim body, comforted by the firmness of her lips, by the familiar smell of her hair.

"Of course we'll come back," I whispered to her. "Dartington will still be here."

She smiled mysteriously, saying nothing.

"We will, won't we?"

"Perhaps," Esther said.

There was no more to say. So, a little later, we got up together and climbed the hill toward the school, laughing.

Patrick Raymond was born in Sussex, England, and was educated at Dartington Hall, where *Daniel and Esther* takes place. After studying briefly at the University of Cape Town in South Africa, he returned to England to serve in the Royal Air Force during World War II. After the war, he served in the Far East, among other places, and in 1977 he retired with the rank of group captain. Patrick Raymond's wartime flying experience provided the background for his adult novel *The White War,* and his travels in the Middle East were the inspiration for his books *The Last Soldier* and *A Matter of Assassination.* Since his retirement from the Royal Air Force, he has continued writing and has developed an interest in gardening, cooking, and painting. *Daniel and Esther* is his first novel for young people.